The Cyber said, "The problem is such that any prediction would be of such a low order of probability as to be almost valueless. The dead man could have come from the vessel; a passenger or a member of the crew. He could have been Dumarest or his companion, Angado. The grave itself need have nothing to with either the ship or the man you are hunting. Coincidences do happen."

Avro remembered the bleak room, the blocks of plastic, the same cold watchful eyes of the tutor. It was tempting to accept the suggestions. Coincidences did happen, but he knew this was not one of them. A conviction on the intuitive level as strong as that which told him Dumarest was still alive.

But where? Where?

E.C. TUBB
has written the following
Dumarest novels for DAW Books:

MAYENNE

JONDELLE

ZENYA

ELOISE

EYE OF THE ZODIAC

JACK OF SWORDS

SPECTRUM OF A FORGOTTEN SUN

HAVEN OF DARKNESS

PRISON OF NIGHT

INCIDENT ON ATH

THE QUILLIAN SECTOR

WEB OF SAND

IDUNA'S UNIVERSE

THE TERRA DATA

WORLD OF PROMISE

NECTAR OF HEAVEN

THE TERRIDAE

THE COMING EVENT

EARTH IS HEAVEN

MELOME

ANGADO

E. C. Tubb

DAW BOOKS, INC.
DONALD A. WOLLHEIM, PUBLISHER

1633 Broadway, New York, NY 10019

To: My mother with love.

First Printing, February 1984

1 2 3 4 5 6 7 8 9

DAW TRADEMARK REGISTERED
U.S. PAT. OFF. MARCA
REGISTRADA. HECHO EN U.S.A.

PRINTED IN U.S.A.

Chapter One

Once, the place had been bright with the froth of make-believe; domes, minarets, spires, towers, soaring arches and sweeping promenades all blazing with variegated colors—a skillful illusion created with paint and plastic, lying like a jewel in the cup of rounded hills. The circus of Chen Wei was gone now, leaving only an expanse of torn and barren ground, a scatter of debris, the crusted surface of a fetid lagoon.

A monument to emotional waste, which Avro pondered as his raft circled the area. How many work-hours had been poured into its construction, operation and maintenance? How many more had been squandered by those visiting the circus for the sake of transient thrills? Time, effort, resources, skills all dissipated to the wind. Leaving nothing but a raw devastation. Time would heal the wound and soon the hills would seem as if they had never been touched. More waste. Under correct guidance things of lasting worth could have been constructed for the benefit of humanity. Testimonials to the efficiency of the Cyclan.

Instead the place was evidence as to its failure.

"Master?" The acolyte was deferential, the title more than an acknowledgment of Avro's superiority. "Would you care to go lower?"

"No." Avro had seen enough. "When did they leave?"

"Five days ago." Cardor added, "A week after the accident."

When Tron had died, and Valaban, and most important of all, Dumarest. Avro looked again at the place where it had happened, assessing, extrapolating, knowing the mental bitter-

5

ness of defeat. Too late. He had arrived too late. A matter of days and his search would have been over, his mission accomplished. Dumarest, taken and helpless in his charge. Dumarest—and the precious secret he owned. One which had made Avro into an angel.

The cyber leaned back as the raft headed toward town. High above, a winged shape glided, others wheeling close. Small birds feeding on airborne seeds, mindless creatures operating on a plane of sheer instinct but, for a moment, he envied them. Remembering the freedom of the skies, the rush of wind, the thrum of pinions, the surging impact of alien emotions. Then he had known hate and fear and anger and, yes, even concern. He had known the burning flame of passion and, at the end, he had experienced death.

Watching him, Cardor felt a mounting unease. He was young, taken and trained by the Cyclan, yet still to don the scarlet robe which was the mark of a cyber. He might never wear it. Not all acolytes made the grade. Some continued to work in subordinate capacities but the majority quietly vanished from sight, erased by the touch of oblivion.

He said, "I did what I could, master. As I was ordered to do."

By Tron who had demonstrated his inefficiency. Who had escaped his punishment by extinction.

"Tell me again what happened."

Unnecessary repetition, every detail was clear in Avro's mind as the acolyte knew. As he also knew that, in making the demand, the cyber had put him on trial. The next few minutes would decide his fate.

"I arrived with Cyber Tron on Baatz fifteen days ago. We stayed at the Dubedat Hotel. He was in contact with an agent in the circus of Chen Wei. The man had reported that Dumarest was attached to the circus and could be captured. Cyber Tron visited the circus but neither Dumarest nor the agent was present. He made a second visit later. That is when he died."

"And you?"

"Obeying orders, I stayed in town. To meet you should you arrive and report on what was happening. When Cyber Tron failed to return I made inquiries at the circus. There I learned of the accident." Cardor paused, reliving the incident, recognizing its importance. "The owner, Tayu Shakira, explained what had happened. An animal had gone berserk, broken free of its cage and had run amok. A klachen. It—''

"I know what it is. Continue."

"Its keeper, Valaban, had been killed. Cyber Tron and Dumarest also. There were witnesses."

"Did you see the bodies?"

"No. But with Shakira's permission I tested the witnesses with lie-detectors. All responses were positive. They were not lying."

"But you did not see the bodies."

"They had been disposed of before I arrived. A matter of necessity, so it was explained. The scent of blood needed to be eradicated in order to prevent further upset among the beasts. And the bodies themselves were terribly mangled. But some things had been saved. Cyber Tron's bracelet and a gun he carried. I recognized them both."

Proof the cyber had died—but the others? Avro stared at distant, wheeling shapes. Valaban, certainly, the man must have died if Dumarest had escaped but, from the evidence, he had joined the others in death. A fact Avro found hard to accept; he did not want to accept. Yet to refute the evidence was to be illogical.

"How many witnesses did you examine?"

"Eight. Three actually saw the incident. The others all saw the bodies and three helped to dispose of them."

"And the owner?"

"He actually saw nothing. Cyber Tron must have contacted the agent direct."

"But you tested him?"

"I did. With his permission after I pointed out how ill advised he would be to make an enemy of the Cyclan. The findings confirmed what he claimed."

Which meant that he had not lied. And yet . . . And yet . . .

"Relate the evidence of those who saw the incident," said Avro. "Individually and in detail."

He sat immobile as he listened to the acolyte. The raft headed toward the sun and warm hues painted his face with red and gold and amber. Colors which accentuated the scarlet of his robe, reflecting brilliantly from the sigil adorning his breast. The Seal of the Cyclan, the symbol of his power. Yet despite the sunlight and the warm tint of his robe a chill rested about him. An aura emphasized by the skull-like contours of his face. One thin to the point of emaciation, the scalp shaven, the deep-set eyes meshed by lines. The visage of a living machine devoid of the capacity of emotion. A flesh and blood robot who could only know the pleasure of mental achievement.

Behind him the site of the circus fell away. The barren ground, the litter, the crusted lagoon. The pool in which the dead had been buried and, with them, the ending of a dream.

At night Baatz became a world of gaiety with bright lanterns illuminating the tiered buildings and the market itself turned into a playground. Here the venders, traders, merchants and entrepreneurs put aside business and joined with stallholders, farmers, shopkeepers, housewives, workers and the restless tide of transients that made up the population.

A time of drinking and dancing and merriment but one free of violence. The air saw to that, the invisible spores it carried from the vegetation clothing the surrounding hills. Exudations which calmed and reduced tension so that men laughed instead of quarreling and sought peaceful solutions instead of bloody settlements.

Like a scarlet ghost Avro moved through the town.

Cardor could have accomplished the task, as could others of his own acolytes, but he needed to do it himself. The woman who answered his knock frowned as she saw his face, became respectful as she recognized his robe. Even on Baatz the Cyclan was known.

"My lord!" Her head dipped in a bow. "This is an honor. How may I serve you?"

"A man stayed here." Avro's tone was the even modulation of his kind, devoid of all irritating factors. "Dumarest. Earl Dumarest. I have the correct address?"

"You have, my lord. He hired a room upstairs. In the back." She blinked sorrowful eyes. "Such a pity he died."

"You heard?"

"From the circus. They told me to sell his things and to let the room if anyone wanted it. Not that he'd used it much."

"Let me see it."

It was a box containing a narrow bed, a cabinet, a small

table, two chairs. A rug half-covered the bare wood of the floor. A jug held scummed water and a bowl had a chipped rim. Avro assessed this at a glance then he was at the cabinet, searching, the table, the drawers. They yielded nothing and he dropped to his knees and checked the underside of the bed, the chairs, finally stripping the cot and examining the bare, wooden structure.

Nothing aside from a few crumpled papers, some packets of dried fruit, a book, a folder of bright pictures, a deck of cards. These things he checked with minute attention, holding each of the pasteboards to the light, running his fingers over their edges. Finally he turned his attention to the room itself, scanning each wall, the ceiling, the floor bared when he moved aside the rug.

Again he found nothing and stood, thoughtful, trying to put a man into the chamber, trying to guess what that man would do.

Guessing, for he lacked data on which to base an extrapolation. The essential ingredient to promote his honed talent. Given a handful of facts he could predict the logical outcome of any event; without them he could only make assumptions. A man, alone on a strange world—how would he have safeguarded his secret?

Again Avro checked the room, looking for the fifteen symbols which would tell him all he needed to know: the sequence in which the biomolecular units of the affinity twin had to be assembled. The secret which would give the Cyclan galactic domination.

But he looked for it without success.

A failure he had expected, yet to have ignored the possibility of success would have been insane stupidity. An error equal in magnitude to that made by Tron. To have had Dumarest in his grasp and then to have lost him. Death had been a merciful punishment.

Avro looked once more at the room. A small, bare place, cold, featureless. One Dumarest had known as he must have known so many others. Moving on to leave nothing of himself behind. And yet there had to be more.

He found it at a local bank, the manager reluctant to cooperate, finally yielding to logical persuasion. To refuse Avro's demand was to ruin all hope of promotion.

"Yes," he admitted. "Dumarest did have money on deposit here. Quite a large sum as a matter of fact."

"Withdrawals?"

"None after the initial deposit."

"How was the credit registered?"

"The usual way." The manager added an explanation. "This is a transient world and we get all types. This bank is affiliated with others and we use the common system. When a deposit is made—" He broke off as Avro lifted a hand. "I see you understand."

"Give me the number of the account."

The deposit Dumarest had made had been registered in a pattern of metallic inks set invisibly beneath the skin of his left arm. Special machines could read the code and adjust the credit as necessary. A blast of flame would incinerate the limb had there been any tampering or forgery.

"Here." The manager handed over the desired information. "But no withdrawals have been made to date."

With Dumarest dead none ever would. More proof as to his extinction—would a man in need refuse to use the money that was his?

From the bank Avro went to the field where Cardor waited. The acolyte shook his head in a gesture of defeat.

"Nothing, master. The traffic is too great. It is impossible to gain detailed records of who traveled where and on what vessel."

"The circus?"

"Bound for Lopakhin."

Traveling in assorted ships, some members going their own way, others ready to disperse. All could be followed but nothing new would be gained. Dumarest was dead. All the evidence proved it. To deny the facts was to demonstrate his inefficiency.

Yet to accept evidence without checking was to do the same.

Avro said, "Take men out to the circus lagoon. Have it dragged. If bodies are found have them placed in cryosacs for later examination. Bones also. Nothing must be missed."

"Yes, master." The acolyte hesitated. "But all waste from the circus was pulverized before being pumped to the lagoon."

"Do as I order."

The tone of Avro's voice did not change but Cardor flinched as he bowed and hurried away. A mistake and one he must have recognized; no assumption could be regarded as proof. Yet it was a natural one for him to make, for what else was a dead body but waste? And he had been influenced by Tron who had demonstrated his weakness by his failure.

All this Avro considered as he made his way to the Dubedat Hotel. To waste a valuable resource was to be avoided and the young man could be salvaged. A period of intense training, exposure to what a true cyber could be, a final warning to stiffen his resolve and he could yet earn the right to don the scarlet robe.

A decision made and set to one side as he entered his suite. Byrne rose to greet him, Tupou at his side. Personal aides who have traveled with him.

To them both Avro said, "Total seal."

He moved on, into his chamber, the door closing behind him. A barrier the acolytes would protect with their lives. One enhanced as he touched the broad band of metal clasped to his left wrist. A twin to one Tron had worn; activated, it emitted a pattern of forces which formed a zone impenetrable to any prying electronic eye or ear.

Avro lay supine on his bed.

The hotel was luxurious, the bed soft, the ceiling decorated with intricate designs picked in red and yellow and vivid scarlet. Patterns which vanished as he closed his eyes and concentrated on the Samatchazi formula. Gradually he lost the use of his senses; had he opened his eyes he would have been blind. Divorced of external stimuli his brain ceased to be irritated, gained tranquility and calm, became a thing of pure intellect, its reasoning awareness the only thread with normal existence. Only then did the grafted Homochon elements become active. Rapport was immediate.

It was followed by chaos.

Avro felt the mental shock and twisted in his mind, screaming as his body lay immobile on the bed, dumb, soundless, incapable of movement. A husk that housed roiling insanity, a conflict of jarring discord, flashes of light, of color, of searing impossibility. A turmoil in which he spun like a leaf in a gale, helpless to do other than ride the storm, to wait for a period of calm.

It came with the echoes of rolling thunder yielding to a host of twitterings, whispers, murmurings, sighs. A shadowed darkness which slowly brightened to reveal a bizarre landscape composed of crystalline facets gleaming with a fire of splintered colors. A ball in which he stood with his feet resting on softly engulfing shadows.

Before him stood a mirror image of himself.

A shape as tall, as thin, as skeletal about the face. One wearing the twin of his scarlet robe. But the image was no reflection and he recognized it at once. Master Marle, Cyber Prime, the head of the Cyclan.

But how? How?

Normally communication with Central Intelligence was preceded by the illusion of bubbles moving in continuous motion with other bubbles all composed of gleaming light. An experience unique to himself; each cyber had a different experience. Then would come the actual contact during which information was absorbed from his mind as water was sucked by a sponge from a pool. An interchange in which orders were relayed as fast. Organic communication of a near-instantaneous speed. After would come the time of euphoria in which he drifted in a zone filled with the scraps of overflow from other minds.

Never before had he known this confusion.

"Avro?" Marle sounded as confused as himself. "Are you Avro?"

"Marle?" Avro caught himself, the evidence was before him. Incredible as it seemed they stood face to face. "A coincidence," he suggested. "We both established rapport at the same time and Central Intelligence has created this direct link. An improvement if restricted to special occasions."

"Perhaps." Marle was slow to agree. "What have you to report?"

"Dumarest is dead."

"Explain." Marle listened as Avro gave him the facts. "The lagoon?"

"Can only produce negative evidence. Anything recovered may, on examination, prove the death of Tron of which we have no doubt. The rest must be based on a valuation of other evidence. I regard it as conclusive."

"Eye-witness accounts," said Marle. "Irrefutable testimony substantiated by mechanical lie-detectors. And yet you were not satisfied."

"I needed to be certain."

"Of what? To check the lagoon was wasted effort if you believe the testimony. Time and expense used to no purpose. Could Cardor have lied?"

"No. His findings have been checked."

"So he told the truth as he knew it. As others could have done."

Avro caught the implication and stepped forward, noting, with vague detachment, that the figure he faced remained at the same distance.

He said, "The possibility that a man could lie and yet not know that he lied is credible. Hypnotism could produce such a condition. But there were eight witnesses, not including the owner of the circus. All eight had seen the bodies and all swore as to the deaths. Also Cardor took steps to guard against such conditioning. I have checked the detectors and the results are conclusive. The men saw what they claimed to have seen."

"Tron dead? Valaban?"

"And Dumarest. All three the victims of a klachen which had run wild."

"And the animal?"

Avro hesitated. "Dead, I think."

"You are not positive?"

"No mention was made of it. The fate of the beast was not considered important."

Against the greater loss that was understandable but it was an oversight which could not be forgiven. Avro revised his decision as to Cardor's fate. He would be questioned, tested, checked—then disposed of. Marle, by his question, had cost the man his life.

As, by his decision, he could cost Avro his.

As Avro watched, the figure before him seemed to blur, to dissolve into smoke which writhed and plumed to dissipate against the bizarre landscape. An illusion added to illusion, or reality which his limited senses could only convert to familiar terms. Then the return of the wind, the confusion, the mind-wrenching turmoil as the universe gyrated around him and his ears were filled with the thin, hopeless screaming of the damned.

"Master!" Someone was pounding at the door. "Master! Is all well?"

Byrne, his face anxious as Avro broke the total seal, Tupou behind him carrying wine. Ruby fluid which he gushed into a goblet and handed to Avro without a word. Liquid he drank without thinking then dismissed them both with a curt gesture. Alone, he sank on the bed and buried his face in his hands.

And heard the song of wind, the thrum of pinions, the thin, keen hiss of parting air.

Madness and he reared, looking at the walls, the ceiling, the familiar shapes of ornate furnishings. Things to be despised for their nonfunctional design but now objects of comfort.

What had happened?

Coincidence, Marle had said, or the figure he had taken to be the Cyber Prime. But it was a coincidence which must have happened many times before. Why had this been different?

Avro examined the problem with trained mental efficiency.

Central Intelligence was the sum total of the massed brains which formed the heart of the Cyclan. Living intelligences, released from the hampering prisons of fleshy bodies when age had made those bodies no longer efficient. Locked in sealed capsules, fed with nutrients, hooked in series, the brains rested in darkness and total isolation from external stimuli. An ideal state in which to ponder the problems of the universe. A tremendous organic computer of incredible complexity; with its aid the Cyclan would rule the galaxy given time.

But the tool had revealed a flaw. Certain of the brains had shown signs of aberrated behavior and had to be destroyed. Was the sickness continuing?

Was Central Intelligence going insane?

A possibility loaded with frightening implications, for if the brains could no longer be trusted then what of the Cyclan? And what would be the reaction of cybers denied their reward for dedicated service? The potential immortality granted at the end of their useful physical life?

"Master!" Byrne turned as Avro opened the door to his chamber. "Is all well?"

A question Avro dismissed with a wave of his hand.

"Go to the field," he ordered. "I want all details of every vessel movement from Baatz from the time Tron landed here. Names, cargoes, destinations, complements, operating velocities—everything." To Tupou he said, "Bring all the records of the examinations made by Cardor together with a complete record of all circus workers." A near-impossible task but one which had to be attempted. "When you have done that, relieve Cardor and have him report to me."

Effort and expense with little hope of reward but Avro was beyond counting the cost. If Dumarest was dead he must be certain of it. If, despite all the evidence, the man had managed to survive then he must know that too. The future of the Cyclan depended on it.

Chapter Two

From his seat at the table Helith Lam looked at the prospects in the salon. They weren't encouraging, the usual assortment of deadbeats and cheap riders, but he had a place to fill and Krogstad was getting ugly. The gambler thinned his lips at recent memory, seeing the captain's face in his mind's eye, the cruel, determined set of the mouth. The ultimatum had been brief.

"Up the take or quit the *Thorn*!"

Dumped on Cadell or Bilton or another of the small worlds forming the Burdinnion. Garbage dumps mostly with little trade, no industry, scant farming and a viciously savage native life. Once kicked off the *Thorn* on such a world and he would starve. Too old to sell his labor, too inexperienced to wrest a living from the local terrain, he'd last only as long as his money. And the captain, damn him, would leave little of that.

A bleak prospect and one he had to improve. A decent cut from the table would grant him a reprieve and he could pad the captain's fifty percent share of the profit from his own cut. But first he had to fill the vacant seat.

"Come on!" Lissek, seated to his left, was impatient. "You're letting the deck grow cold."

"It'll warm." Cranmer was cynical. "Why be in a hurry to lose your money?"

"That's right." Varinia touched a handkerchief to lips painted a lurid scarlet. "Why be in a hurry over anything? But why the delay?"

"We need seven," said Lam. A lie and one he justified.

"It makes a better game and adds spice. Also it brings in fresh money."

"You should have told that to Deakin before he got skinned." Yalin, a wasp of a man, rapped a finger on the coins piled before him. "Come on, man, deal!"

Lam obeyed; a moving game attracted attention but his eyes weighed those lounging in the salon. The monk was out; no Brother of the Universal Church would waste time and money at the table. The young married couple had other things to interest them; after they'd swallowed their ration of basic they would vanish into their cabin. The gaunt-faced seller of symbiotes was immersed in his books and the old woman with the artificial gems had already used up her luck. Which left only two others.

"Damn!" A raddle-faced miner swore and threw down his hand. "That decides it! I'm out!"

"And me." A pale youngster followed his example. "Varinia?"

"Stays," said Lam, then, softening his tone, added with a smile, "We need her to make up the number and to add a touch of beauty to the company. And I don't think she'll regret it. See?" The cards riffled in his hands, falling to lie face upward. "Four Lords—could you hope for better? Your luck is about to change, my dear."

"It had better." Her eyes met his in mutual understanding. "But who else will join us?"

"Our friends." Lam lifted his voice as he made the appeal. "Please, you two, accommodate us. A small game to while away the time." Then, as the younger of the pair turned toward him, "Angado Nossak, isn't it? I think we have met before."

"On the *Provost*," agreed Nossak. "You taught me a hard lesson. Maybe now's the time to put it to use."

He took a chair, gesturing for his companion to take another. A hard man, decided the gambler, looking at him. A brief glance but enough to take in the shape and build. Faded garments spoke of hard times and the shiny patches on the fabric showed where straps could have hung or accoutrements rested. A mercenary, he guessed, a professional guard or a hunter—now down on his luck and hoping to improve it.

A forlorn hope, as was Nossak's intention to use what he

had learned. Both prime fodder for the gambler's art and he riffled the cards, the rubbed-down skin of index fingers and thumbs reading the tiny marks a nail had impressed into the edges.

"Well, my lords and lady—" he inclined his head toward Varinia—"let us begin."

The game was starburn; a variation of poker with a seven-card deal and a double discard dropping the hand to the normal five cards. Lissek sucked in his breath as he scooped up his hand, a thin stream of purple running from the corner of his mouth. Saliva stained by the weed he chewed to ease his cough and steady his nerves.

"Give me three." He dropped five cards on the table. "Make them friendly."

So he had a pair. Lam glanced at Cranmer. Dealt him two cards, moved to where Nossak studied his hand.

"Three—no! Make it two." He watched Lam deal. "Earl?"

"I'll take one."

Dumarest watched as the deal moved on to the woman, his eyes on the gambler's hands. Smooth, ringless, the skin soft and supple. The result of applied salves, he guessed. He was certain as to why the index fingers and thumbs lacked any trace of the normal whorls and patterns.

A cheat and a desperate one; the risks he took were obvious. Chances he compounded as he returned to Lissek who threw down two cards for another pair. His original hand had been improved to one containing three of a kind, now, with luck, he could have built it into a full house or gained a healthy four. Cranmer shook his head after the final deal and dropped out. Angado pursed his lips and changed a single card. Dumarest shook his head and threw in his hand. The woman stayed. The gambler. Three rounds of betting and the game was over.

Varinia chuckled as she scooped in the pot.

"You know, Lam, I think I'm going to like this game."

One designed to build the pot and to ruthlessly squeeze the players. The extra cards and double discarding enabled good hands to be won and encouraged pressure-betting. If the dealer could manipulate the cards he would find it simple to clean up.

Lam could manipulate them and was clever despite his

desperation. He was using the woman as his shill, letting her win so as to cover his own involvement. Later, when she had grown too confident, he would clean her out.

"Raise ten." Angado threw coins into the pot. "This time I win."

Dumarest doubted it but made no comment. The man was his cabin mate, a temporary association born of chance. He owed the man nothing and his main concern was to remain inconspicuous. He'd left Baatz in a crate supplied by the circus, transported by discreet friends of the owner, shipped by a captain who wasn't too curious.

A journey ending with Dumarest in a warehouse. One he'd broken out of to take passage on a vessel heading toward the Burdinnion. Changing to the *Thorn* on Tysa. A ship like most in the region, catering to all trades, making short journeys, touching small and almost deserted worlds.

Now he had to make a decision. If Angado continued to play he would lose and could become violent, which would bring attention not only to himself but to the man who shared his cabin. But to beat the gambler at his own game would be to arouse a more direct interest.

And the captain was no fool.

Ships, even battered tubs like the *Thorn*, were valuable possessions and all took elementary precautions. A man who lied could be harmless but no harmless man had reason to lie. Dumarest had maintained his deception by giving only half his name but a deeper check would reveal things he wanted to keep hidden.

"You in?" Angado Nossak was impatient, sweating, hand tugging at the collar of his blouse. "God, it's hot in here. Where's the steward? I want some ice."

"Hot?" The gambler looked puzzled. "I've noticed no change." He looked at Dumarest. "You in or out?"

"In." Dumarest chipped into the pot. "No raise."

Varinia hesitated, glanced at Lam, then doubled Nossak's raise. Pressure which drove out Lissek and Cranmer. Nossak hesitated as he examined his hand, pulling at his collar and finally tearing open his blouse.

"I'm burning. Where's that damned steward?"

"Forget him." Varinia stared at the man. "You sick or

something?'' Her voice rose in sudden fear. ''Hell, man, look at your face!''

It had broken out in lumpy protrusions. An attack shocking in the speed of its progression. The woman jumped up and backed from the table, others following, cards spraying from the gambler's hand as Nossak slumped over the table. Within seconds Dumarest was alone with the sick man in a circle of staring faces.

''Get the steward,'' said Lissek. ''He'll know what to do. He's got drugs.''

''Drugs, hell!'' Cranmer was harshly aggressive. ''Get the captain. That man's got plague!''

Captain Krogstad took five paces over the floor of the salon, turned, paced back to where he had started. Aside from himself, Brother Jofre and his first officer, the place was deserted. All the passengers were safely locked in their cabins and he wished Jofre was among them. But he knew better than to be hostile. It didn't pay to ride roughshod over the Universal Church.

He said, ''Brother, you must see the situation from my point of view. As captain I am responsible for the ship and all in it. I cannot permit the possibility of contagion to remain.''

''You are assuming the sick man is a carrier of disease. That need not be the case.''

Krogstad was blunt. ''With respect, Brother, you are not a medical man. I can't afford to take a chance on your diagnosis. If you are wrong—''

''Then the damage has already been done.'' The monk met the captain's eyes. ''The ship has become infected and your duty is clear. All must be placed under total quarantine. You must send word to your world of destination for ships to monitor the isolation of the *Thorn* while in orbit. It will have to remain in that condition until such time as a clearance is granted.''

Which would take its own sweet time, as Krogstad knew. Time during which expenses would mount from feeding the passengers and crew, from medical fees and the charges made by the monitors. Costs which would eat into his reserves and could leave him ruined.

Fedotik, the first officer, cleared his throat.

"There is an alternative," he suggested. "The sick man can be kept isolated, evicted if he dies." Or even if he doesn't—who would be concerned over the fate of a single man? Something which would already have been done if it hadn't been for Jofre's presence. "I'm thinking of the best for everyone," he added. "As you must be. It is our duty to safeguard the welfare of the majority."

"Not at the expense of the minority." Jofre was firm. "I don't think isolation is the answer."

"What else can we do?" Again Krogstad paced the floor. "Quarantine would ruin us and once I send the word there can be no retraction. If—" He halted and snapped his fingers. "I have it. The sick man is not alone. His cabin mate is with him. If Nossak is diseased with a contagious illness then his companion must be affected. As yet he appears untouched. Which must be evidence of a harmless infection."

"The man could be a carrier."

Fedotik said, quickly, "We have considered the possibility and have a solution which we hope will meet with your approval. The ship is bound for Anfisa. We can make a diversion and land on Velor away from any habitable area." He saw Jofre's expression and added, "Not too far away, of course, and we can leave supplies. If the illness is harmless—as we are certain it is—then they will recover and no harm will have been done."

"And the ship will be safe," said Krogstad. "By the time we reach Anfisa we'll know for sure if any plague is on board. If there is more sickness the authorities will be notified." He spread his hands in mute appeal. "Two men against the ruin of us all. Brother, I beg you to accept the compromise."

One made only because of his presence. Jofre had no illusions as to the captain's motives. To evict the pair would be easier and cheaper than landing on Velor.

"When?"

"Two days."

"Can I see them?" Jofre listened to the silence which was his answer. "Talk with them?" A pause, then he said firmly, "At least let me check their supplies."

Things Dumarest stacked after the ship had gone, leaving him and the sick man on a rolling plain already touched by shadows. Low on the horizon a sullen sun threw long rays of gold and amber, orange and yellow light, which illuminated drifting cloud to swathe the sky in dying beauty. As the day died so did its heat and Dumarest worked quickly to build a fire, using dried grasses and lumps of peat which burned slowly and cast a somber glow.

"Earl!" Nossak woke to rear upright where he had lain. "Earl!"

"I'm here, Angado." Dumarest handed the man a canteen. "How do you feel?"

"I'm burning. My insides are like a furnace and I ache all over." He drank and fell back to lie in the shelter of the supplies. "So we got dumped, eh? I thought it was a nightmare. Well, I guess it's better than getting thrown into the void. What was it that hit me?"

Dumarest shrugged. "Maybe a virus of some kind or it could have been an allergy. No one seemed to want to find out. That fool Cranmer shouted 'plague' and that was it."

"So I got dumped and you with me." Nossak turned his head, face ugly with lumps now darkened with blotches. "I guess you had no choice, huh?"

"No."

"If you had? I mean, would you be here now?"

"No."

"At least you're honest. I'll have to remember that. Maybe . . ."

He fell back, lost in a sudden sleep which was close to a coma; fitful periods of unconsciousness that hit at any time and without warning. A symptom of his illness; the lumps were another. Blotched masses hard beneath the skin that covered his entire body. Some were crusted by the dried scabs of oozing secretions.

By the light of the fire and the stars overhead Dumarest checked the supplies. There was water, concentrated food, a small supply of drugs, a hand axe, a compass, some needles and thread, a length of fine wire, a knife. Dumarest compared it to the one he lifted from his boot then set it to one side. The rest of the bulk was made up of two large but empty plastic sacs and a bundle of clothing.

Dumarest piled most of them around the sick man, covering the whole with one of the plastic bags. Seated before the fire he worked at the length of wire, fashioning lines ending in running loops. Stepping into the starlit darkness he set the snares, holding them with doubled ends of the wire set deep in the dirt. Back at the fire he ate a wafer of concentrate, washed it down with a sip of water and, knife in hand, closed his eyes.

He slept like an animal, hovering on the brink of wakefulness, starting alert as something threshed in the grass to one side. A small rodent, he guessed, which had become caught in a snare and he mentally marked the direction of the noise.

As the stars began to pale with the onset of dawn he heard a series of dull explosions to the north followed by a vivid lavender flash. He marked it with the knives dug into the ground to form a line of sight which he checked with the compass as the day grew brighter. When the plain lay revealed in sharp detail he went to check the snares, finding them all intact except one. It rested in a twisted mass among crushed grass stained with flecks of blood. Around it he saw the marks of spatulate paws.

An hour later it began to rain.

Angado Nossak was singing in a high, cracked voice, a melody that made little sense followed by a babbling string of words that made even less. Dumarest rose from his place beside the fire and crossed to the prostrate man. It was late afternoon, the rain had cleared the air leaving a brisk freshness now sharpened by the chill of approaching evening.

"Earl!" The babbling stopped as the man looked up, crusted lips parting in a smile. "Good old Earl. My friend. My faithful retainer. Did I tell you how you will be rewarded? For you a palace filled with nubile maidens, fountains of wine, tables groaning beneath the weight of assorted viands. Land and workers to tend your crops. On Lychen you will live like a king."

"Lychen?"

"My home world. The residence of the family to which I belong. Allow me to present Hedren Angado Nossak Karroum." His arm waved in a vague gesture. "The spoiled son of a decaying line. Yet there are those who hold me in high regard. Those who . . . who. . . ."

"Wake up!" The slap of Dumarest's hand against the

lolling cheek caused birds to rise with startled croakings from the plain. "Damn you, wake up!" Another slap. As the eyes opened to focus with bleared concentration Dumarest snapped, "Now listen to me! Listen, damn you! I'm giving you two days to get on your feet. Until the dawn after next. Call it thirty-six hours. Do you understand?"

"Earl, I. . . ."

"Keep awake!" Dumarest rose and gripped the plastic sac he had spread over the recumbent man. The rain it had trapped sloshed wetly over his hands to cascade down over Nossak's face and head; the deluge caused him to splutter but cleared his eyes. "Now listen!"

"Earl?"

"You're ill, dying, and I mean that. Unless you're able to travel the day after tomorrow I'm leaving you. That means you work to get well or you stay and be food for what's living out there." Dumarest jerked his head at the plain. "It's up to you. Personally I don't give a damn. I'd be better off alone."

"You mean it." Nossak struggled to focus his eyes. "You really mean it."

"That's right." Dumarest's tone matched his expression, cold, hard, unyielding. "Now hold still."

The drugs were in ampules fitted with hollow needles serving as strings. The first brought sleep, the second was loaded with wide-coverage antibiotics, the third held slow time; chemical magic which speeded the metabolism and stretched seconds into minutes, hours into days. Angado would wake thin, starving, but able to walk if luck was with him. If his survival instinct, bolstered by the grim warning, gave him the needed incentive. If either failed then he would die.

Dumarest covered the sleeping man with clothing, covered that with one of the plastic sacs and turned away. He'd done all he could and now it was time to ensure his own survival.

Far out on the plain birds rose with a sudden thrum of wings, and he studied them, eyes narrowed as he counted their number, the direction of their flight. A period of quiet and then another sudden uprush of winged shapes, closer and heading in his general direction. More came as the sun touched the horizon much closer than the others. Then nothing but silence and the brooding of watching eyes.

Out on the plain death was waiting.

Dumarest knew what it had to be. In such open country game was scarce and hard to bring down. The creature that had stolen the snared rodent had tasted blood and wanted more. It was only a question of time before the predator decided to attack.

For Dumarest it couldn't be too soon.

He had prepared the trap; ropes woven from strips of clothing now set to form a pattern of loops and barriers that would hamper quick movement if the beast loped over the area. The bait was made of food concentrates pounded and soaked in water thickly stained with his own blood. A compound smeared on a bundle of clothing set near enough to the smoldering fire for the heat to disperse the scent but not too close to frighten the beast away.

Now there was nothing to do but wait and he crouched, waiting, watchful, the small axe to hand, a knife resting in each boot. A man matching his patience against that of a beast, his ability to kill against a creature developed for just that attribute.

The fire dwindled, became a sullen, ashed ball, a shrinking, bloodshot eye. High above, the stars shone with an increasing brightness, a brilliant scatter of glowing points, sheets and curtains of luminescence interspersed with the fuzz of distant nebulae. Suns were close in the Burdinnion and always, toward the galactic center, the skies at night showed a blaze of luminescence, touching the plain with a soft, nacreous glow. Turning dried stems into wands of silver, drooping leaves into fronds of shining, filigreed silk until the frosted landscape stirred to the touch of a gentle wind that filled the air with a whispering susurration.

Dumarest thinned his lips as he stared into the empty spaces.

The wind would mask the approach he'd hoped to catch. The slithering rustle of a creature making its attack. One impossible to avoid and the only warning he would get. Now, because of the wind, his ears were useless and his vision limited. The beast could be behind him at this very moment, crouching, claws ripping into the ground as it sprang, those same claws reaching out to tear the flesh from his bones.

Dumarest dropped, an ear pressed to the ground, the other covered as he strained to catch subtle vibrations. He heard nothing but the beat of his own heart. A hand snatched a knife from his boot, drove it into the dirt, metal jarring against his teeth as he clamped them on the blade. A long, dragging moment then he heard it. A soft rumble, a rasp, a sound more movement than noise. Echoes transmitted through the ground and into the knife and by bone conduction into his brain.

A murmur which grew stronger, closer and then, abruptly, ceased.

Turning, snatching at knife and axe, Dumarest saw it limned against the stars.

A beast like a tiger, five feet long from head to the root of the tail, clawed paws extended, jaws gaping to reveal long, pointed fangs. A ruff of fur circled the neck to run in a line along the back. The tail, like a whip, bore a spined end. The back legs held razors.

Natural weapons which kicked at the ground to throw dirt pluming upward as the jaws closed on the clothing bearing the bait. The snarl of frustrated anger was a guttural roar of muted thunder, and shreds of fabric flew to either side as the beast vented its rage. Then it dropped the rags and stood, snuffing the air, head turning to where Nossak lay in drugged unconsciousness.

Dumarest acted before it could spring.

The axe spun from his hand, whirling to bite into the neck, the blade shearing through hide and muscle but missing the arteries. An attack which confused the animal by its sheer unexpectedness and it sprang to one side, head turning, jaws gaping as it scented the new enemy. One which came darting toward the creature, knives in hand, steel which stung and slashed at tendons and ligaments.

Dumarest moved back and felt the wind as a paw raked at his face. Then he was running, jumping high over the ropes he had set out. Behind him the animal snarled as the strands hampered its movement, a noose tightening to trap a rear leg.

Dumarest returned to the attack. The beast had to be killed, not frightened off to lurk hurt and dangerous on the plain. He darted forward as the animal reared, paws extended, jaws gaping. A lunge which placed him within range of the belly and he felt the jar and rasp as claws tore at his shoulders and back, the impact of the knife as it plunged deep to release a gush of blood.

He twisted as the free rear leg kicked out in a hammer blow which sent him staggering to fall beside the fire.

Rising, he snatched at the coals, threw them, ran toward the beast as sparks coated the snarling mask. His speed sent his face to press against the neck, his head rammed up hard beneath the lower jaw, his left hand rising to grip the mane as his right felt along the cage of the ribs.

To find the pulse of the heart. . . .

Stopped as he drove home his knife.

Chapter Three

Alive!

Avro leaned back in his chair, feeling his mind expand with the euphoria of relief. On the desk before him rested the reports and findings on which he had based his conclusions. They were not certain—nothing could ever be that—but the probability that Dumarest was alive was above ninety percent. And, for him, that was good enough.

The eye-witness reports had given him the initial clue—Cardor had been thorough on that if nothing else. The stories were too similar, not exact, for that would have been obvious, but certain facets had left unanswered doubts. The viewpoints seemed to be roughly the same and that was wrong. The relation placed the same importance on the series of events and that too hadn't quite fit. Yet all was explained if the speakers had, somehow, been influenced by one other. Told the story and been made to believe it to be true. And for them it had been true.

But none had remembered what had happened to the klachen that had run berserk in a killing frenzy.

A mistake and he wondered who had made it. The owner? It was possible but even if true it no longer mattered. Punishment needed to be extracted for Tron's death though it could have been accidental. The animal could have broken free. Could have killed the cyber and the agent, and Dumarest, recognizing his chance, had taken it.

Speculation of no value and Avro dismissed it. The proof was enough and he leaned forward to examine it. The correlated reports, the scraps regained from the lagoon; bones, fragments of clothing, the remains of four bodies, one of them a woman.

The report of a man who had been found drinking in a tavern and telling of a vicious fight in the ring of the circus. A combat Dumarest had won.

The dead man had aided the deception.

Avro picked up a fragment of clothing, gray plastic covering a hidden metal mesh—protection favored by travelers and known to be worn by Dumarest. But such clothing was common, especially among those visiting hostile worlds. Dumarest could already have replaced it if he was alive.

Avro was convinced he was.

His luck would have seen to that. The peculiar ability Dumarest seemed to possess which yielded favorable circumstances when they were most needed. A survival trait Avro had recognized and which must govern his every step in the pursuit of the quarry.

But, if Dumarest was alive, where was he to be found?

The answer lay in the mass of data resting on the desk; the ship movements, cargo manifests, destinations, reports culled from a thousand sources. Most was unrelated trivia but from the rest Avro had selected items which could form a pattern. One which would carry the image of truth.

Baatz was a busy world with traders and merchants coming from all parts to buy and sell in the market. But such could be eliminated; creatures of habit, they were known, their movements predictable. Others posed harder problems, gamblers, harlots, pimps, entrepreneurs together with free-traders and other vessels following no regular routes. Yet the apparent randomness took on a different aspect when the whole was considered. Transient though the population of Baatz might be, yet it followed certain laws similar to those dictating the migrations of birds and wild animals. The need of being at the feeding ground at the right time, the combination of holiday and carnival and the flux of tourists.

Few, like Dumarest, were unattached wanderers drifting from world to world without apparent reason. And those working on the field had grown to recognize the regular visitors.

Avro studied a thin sheaf of reports. A man resembling

Dumarest had taken passage on the *Sinden* a day after Tron had landed. Too soon—eliminate him. Another had left on the *Harrif* a day after the cyber had died. A gambler known to the field agent and expected back soon. Two men who had looked furtive, one who had hidden his face, another traveling with a giggling harlot, a somber individual who wore gray along with the mask of a clown.

A possibility Avro considered then discarded; even if Dumarest had chosen to hide behind conspicuousness the ship had been bound for Zshen. A long flight. Too long for a man needing to lose himself.

And there were other factors to be taken into account. Central Intelligence absorbed an astronomical amount of information from a host of cybers. Data of no obvious value but all taken and sifted through the organic computer to be correlated, aligned, evaluated and all possible connections checked and determined.

Information passed to Avro at his request.

He stared at the papers before him, remembering, wondering why, the last time he had established rapport, it had been as normal. There had been no bizarre landscape, no figure to greet him and exchange words as if face to face. No enclosed universe in which he had been thrust as if by a whim. Would it ever happen again?

He set aside that question as he returned to his task. With a handful of facts he could predict the logical outcome of any event. Training and talent which could not only show where Dumarest had been but predict where he would be and when.

On Nyne a warehouse had been damaged. Broken out of by someone locked within. An item of local news coupled with that of a broken crate. And crates of just that size had been shipped from Baatz after Tron had died. Dumarest could have traveled in one. And after?

The Burdinnion was close and a good place for a man to hide. Easy traveling, with journeys too short to do other than ride Middle. Natural time spent in a variety of ways all designed to eliminate boredom—and Dumarest had skill as a gambler.

Which ship and where headed?

Three had left Nyne at the relevant time. One, a private

charter, could be eliminated; such craft didn't cater to the casual trade. Another, heading toward Baatz, the same. The third, the *Solinoy*, had been bound for Tysa.

Tysa?

It held nothing but a farming complex fueling a stringent economy based on the export of medicinal drugs. A small, harsh, bleak world lashed by radiation and populated mostly by contract workers who had no choice but to stay where fate had dumped them. The last place a man would hide.

And yet?

Avro checked the data; the mechanism of his mind evaluated probabilities. Then he judged time and distance. A button sank beneath a finger as he reached a decision.

"Master!" Tupou answered the command. "Your orders?"

"Go to the field. Have my ship readied for immediate flight. I shall require full velocity. Have Byrne clear the suite."

"Yes, Master. The destination?"

"Anfisa."

It had to be Anfisa. The *Thorn* had left soon after the *Solinoy* had landed and the ship was bound for that world.

Avro intended to meet it.

Angado Nossak sucked at a bone and said, "Earl, I've never felt better in my life."

He looked it. The lumpy protrusions had gone as had a slight plumpness at the waist and jowls. The skin and eyes were clear. Sitting cross-legged before the fire he was the picture of health.

Dumarest said, "You were lucky."

"Sure I was lucky—I had you to look after me." Nossak sobered as he reached for another meaty bone from the heap stacked before the fire. "Though I had a bad dream, once. A nightmare, I guess. I seemed to hear you saying you were going to desert me."

"It was no dream!"

"It had to be!"

"Is that what you always say when you bump up against something you don't like?" Dumarest lowered the tunic he was working on with plastic and a hot iron; the knife included in the supplies which he'd heated in the fire. "Pretend it doesn't exist? Call it a dream? Keep that up and you won't have to worry about growing old."

"I almost didn't." Nossak looked at his arms and frowned. "You gave me slow time, right?"

"That and other things."

"Drugs, sure, but what about the rest? I'm in too good a shape to have starved for over a month. We've no equipment or supplies for intravenous feeding so how did you manage?"

With blood mixed with water and fed into his stomach through a pipe made from the intestines of the predator. Fluids followed by raw, pulped liver and other soft meats.

Nossak gulped as he listened.

"Maybe I shouldn't have asked."

"Squeamish?"

"Let's just say I was never used to things like that."

"What were you used to?" Dumarest thrust the knife back into the fire. Stripped to shorts his body showed a pattern of bruises, marks left by the blow and rake of claws, the snap of teeth. Only the metal protection of his clothing had saved him from fatal lacerations. Now, slowly, he was doing his best to refurbish the garments. "Servants? Money? Adulation?"

"Let's forget it."

"No." Dumarest's tone brooked no argument. "I want to know. Someone tried to kill you and I got mixed up in it. They could try again. It would help to know why."

"Kill me? But I was sick, ill—"

"Poisoned." Smoke rose as Dumarest applied the hot metal, forcing molten plastic into the rents left by claws. "Nothing crude and it couldn't be detected but it exploded allergic reactions once triggered. Anything could have done it, the cards, the basic, the woman's perfume. What do you know about Cranmer?"

"Nothing. Why?"

"He yelled plague and scared the hell out of everyone. Stopped them thinking, too. A smart assassin would have thought of that. One way or another he wanted you dead. Why?"

"It doesn't matter." Nossak gnawed at the bone. "It happened. It's over. Forget it."

"You said that before."

"Then why not do it?"

Dumarest rose, standing upright, the early sun touching his skin and accentuating the bruises. He dressed, adjusting tunic and pants, slipping his knife into his right boot. The other, the one he had used to melt the plastic, he threw into the dirt at Nossak's feet.

"You'd better have that. The axe I'll take with a canteen, one of the sacs and half the snares. The compass too and some of the concentrates." Stooping, Dumarest lifted a joint of meat from where it had been set to cure in the smoke from the fire. "You can have the rest."

"You're going?"

"Yes."

"But—" Nossak rose to his feet, the bone falling from his hand. "You're leaving me? Earl, you can't do that!"

"Watch me."

"But why? What the hell have I done?"

"Nothing. You're a full-grown man now and can stand on your own. If you can't then too bad—I'm no nursemaid."

Nossak said, slowly, "It's because I won't talk, is that it? But what difference does it make? A man's business is his own affair."

"Not when it involves others. I'm here because of you, remember. I'd like to know why." Dumarest paused then said, flatly, "It's up to you, Angado. Or should it be Hedren? Or Karroum?"

"You know?"

"You babbled. Big promises, long names, great rewards. What's so special about being Hedren Angado Nossak Karroum?"

"The seventh," said Nossak bitterly. "Don't forget the number. And if you want you can stick a title in front. Lord Hedren—" He broke off and spat. "To hell with it. Why can't I have one name like you, Earl?"

"You can. Pick one. Angado. From now on that's it." Dumarest sat and picked up the bone the other had dropped. Handing it back he said. "Eat. We can't afford to waste a thing. Now why would anyone want to see you dead?"

"I don't know."

Dumarest sighed. "Just talk," he suggested. "Fill me in on your background."

It was much what he'd expected, an old and established family suffering from inbreeding and decay. The sharp edge which had originally lifted them to power and carved a position of authority weakened by petty rivalries and jealousy. Angado, the seventh to hold the name and title, had an ambitious cousin. One who had made him a tempting offer.

"Just to travel," said Angado. "A regular income paid as long as I stayed away from home. I could go where I liked, do as I liked, but only on that condition. So you see why the very thought of anyone wanting to kill me is ridiculous."

A fool—as he had shown at the card table; any child could have computed the logical outcome of such an arrangement. One fee paid to a skilled assassin and no more payments. No threat of the wanderer's return. No focus for any dissatisfied associates to use as the basis of a rebellion.

"Perotto is hard but fair," said Angado. "He made a bargain and will stick to it. I'd stake my life on that."

He had and almost lost. Dumarest said, casually, "Is Lychen your home world?"

"Yes, do you know it?"

"I've heard of it."

From Shakira of the circus of Chen Wei. The name of the planet on which he could find someone able and willing to help him to find Earth.

They headed out at noon, moving toward the north where Dumarest had seen the lavender flash. Behind them the fire sent up a thin column of smoke which he used to check their direction.

As it finally fell below the horizon Angado said, "Well, if they ever come looking for us, they'll never find us now."

"No one will come looking."

"I suppose not. Krogstad didn't strike me as the sort of captain who'd burn atoms unless he was paid." Angado shrugged and looked around. "A hell of a place."

The plain stretched around them on all sides. Flat, gently undulating, covered with thick grass, featureless.

Dumarest halted to sniff at the wind. It came from the east, a soft breeze which barely moved the tufted tips of the grass, and the odors it carried were the same as those all around. At a distance birds rose, wheeling, settling as he watched.

"Too far." Angado had misread his interest. "We'd never be able to bring them down." He grunted as Dumarest made no comment. "You ever hunted?"

"At times."

"Big game hunting?"

"Not if I could avoid it."

"There's a thrill to it," said Angado. "Pitting your wits and skill against something which could tread you into the ground if given the chance. Standing, waiting, finger on the trigger. Holding your aim and watching for that one moment to fire. It gets you, Earl. Like a fire in the blood." He frowned as Dumarest remained silent. "If you've hunted you must know what I'm talking about."

Dumarest said, "Did you hunt for food?"

"Of course not. It was for sport."

"Butchery, you mean. Killing for the pleasure of it. Standing in a hide and waiting for the beaters to drive the creature toward you. Waiting for it with a gun. What chance did it have?" Dumarest looked at his companion. "I've seen it. Spoiled bastards, rich, pampered, having fun. They don't see what they leave behind. The hurt beasts, wounded by too hasty a shot, dragging themselves away with their guts trailing after them. Some with broken legs or no leg at all. Animals blinded and left to starve. Hunting! Don't boast to me about hunting!"

"It wasn't like that."

"How do you know? You hired men to clean up the mess but did they do it? Did you check or were you too busy showing off your trophy?"

Angado said, "I'm sorry. I didn't know you felt that way about it. I guessed you were a hunter and you killed that beast—"

"For food and because it threatened us." Dumarest added, "There's a difference. By the time this trip is over you may recognize it."

They moved on over the plain, which was as featureless as a sea. Only the compass kept them on a straight line; without it they would have wandered in circles despite the guiding light of the sun. As it swung toward the horizon Dumarest looked for somewhere to camp. It had to be soon; Angado was showing signs of distress but refused to give in to his weakness. A stubborn man who insisted on gathering fuel for the fire and was reluctant to take his share of water.

"We ought to save it, Earl. Ration it."

"Ration it, yes, but not save it," Dumarest tried to explain. "It's best to store it in our bodies not in a canteen. The same with food. We need all the energy we can get and all the strength. If a chance comes we must be strong enough to take it."

"A chance?"

"For food, water, anything which could help us to survive. This plain can't go on forever. Drink up, now."

Later, when the stars glowed above, he studied the sleeping figure of the younger man. One maybe a decade younger than himself but centuries his junior in experience. A man cosseted when young, spoiled by fawning servants, convinced by his peers that he was not like the majority. The product of wealth and influence who had much to learn. With luck he would learn it before he died.

Dumarest wished they had never met.

Rising he looked toward the north hoping for more of the reports, the lavender flash. He saw nothing but the stars and a rising mist which blurred their light. One which thickened into a fog which closed around like a wall of growing darkness. From it, to the west, he heard a shrill screaming and he added more fuel to the fire.

"Earl?" The screaming had awakened Angado and he reared, voice anxious. "What's that?"

"A hunter at work."

"A predator? Like the one you killed?"

"Maybe."

"Do you think it will attack us?"

"It might."

Angado rose and came to sit with Dumarest at the fire. As he settled he said, "You don't like me, do you? On the

ship it didn't matter, we were just passing strangers, but
here it's different. You told me about the hunting but what
else is wrong? My title?''

"You were born to it."

"And so can't be blamed. Right? Any more than a slave
can be blamed for being a slave. We don't use them on
Lychen, you know. Contract workers, yes, but not slaves.
In the old days we had them but not for a long time now."
Angado held out his hands to the fire. "I guess that's what
you'd call progress."

"Would you?"

"What else? There's a difference between being a slave
and being a contract worker. Workers are in it from choice."

"Unless they owe money," reminded Dumarest. "Or
were sold under sentence."

"Sure—but you aren't saying a man should get away
with crime? And even they get treated well; food, shelter,
clothing, some amusements. It can't be such a bad life."

"Would you want it?" Then, as Angado made no answer
Dumarest said, "For most it's a life sentence. The food, the
shelter, the clothing, all has to be paid for and the company
sets the price. A few amusements and the worker is back
where he started and often worse than before. It takes a rare
type to buy himself free."

"Maybe, but it's still better than slavery. That's why I
said we'd progressed on Lychen. We gave that up a long
time ago."

"Most civilized worlds are against the use of slaves,"
said Dumarest. "Especially those with a high technology.
But it isn't because of a liberal attitude toward freedom.
That's just the reason they like to give to cover the real
motivations."

"Which are?"

"Two. The first is fashion. Once it becomes unfashionable
then a slave owner is at a disadvantage. He will be ostracized,
derided, made to feel socially inferior. His business will
suffer and he'll be hit where it hurts. Once he feels the
pain in his wallet he'll join the rest as a matter of survival.
He'll free his slaves and begin charging them for what he'd
been supplying for nothing. An advantage he'll be quick to
recogonize."

Angado nodded. "That's one reason. The other?"

"A matter of economics. Slaves make bad workers and who can blame them? The higher the technology the less productive they are and the greater the risk of damage to expensive equipment. In the end, to be efficient, you'd need an overseer for each worker. If the overseer can do the job why go to the expense of keeping a slave?"

"Because you can—"

"What? Beat them? Force them to work? Make them obedient? That may be true but you can't force anyone to be clever or loyal or even trustworthy. And what incentive can you give a slave? Freedom? Do that and you lose valuable property. You can kill them, sure, but you'd be hurting yourself in the long run. So it comes back to economics. The only real—" Dumarest broke off, listening, as another thin screaming echoed through the night. "It's made another kill. Good."

"Because now it won't be hungry and so will leave us alone?"

"You're learning."

"More than you think. What were you going to say just then? About slaves. The only real reason anyone would want to own them."

Dumarest hadn't said that but he answered the question.

"Power. Real power. Wealth and influence doesn't make you strong, it only shows how weak others can be. You can bribe them to obey but, if they've any guts, they can always tell you to go to hell. But a slave has no choice. He jumps when you give the word or you have him flogged, burned, tortured, maimed. Power like that can be a drug. Some can't live without it."

Perotto for one as Angado knew. Larsen for another and he saw their faces painted against the mist. Both of equal age, his cousin old enough to be his father. Older than his years, his face seamed with lines of determination, eyes hard beneath thick brows. Had he gone back on his word? Larsen might have dropped the hint with his cunning serpent's tongue, but surely Perotto would never have agreed. Had Larsen acted on his own? If . . .

"Angado, you'd better finish your sleep."

"What?" He blinked at Dumarest. "Sorry, but I was thinking," he said. "Family business."

Of which Dumarest could have no part and yet if it hadn't been for his companion he would be dead by now. Could still die—how long could they hope to survive in this wilderness?

Chapter Four

Halting, Dumarest threw back his head and sniffed at the air. Like a dog, thought Angado dispassionately. Like the animal he'd become as they made their way over the endless plain. Sniffing for scent, looking for sign, surviving where no ordinary man could have lasted. A trait he envied while knowing he could never hope to emulate it.

He stumbled, feeling the jar in knees and hips as he fought to regain his balance. The pack he carried was a monstrous hand pressing him down, a load full of trivia which Dumarest refused to discard. He turned to look behind, seeing their trail wending over the rolling plain toward a featureless horizon, one which faded, vanishing, as gusting wind flurried the long grass and resettled it in a new pattern.

The trail they left was as transient as that made by a boat on an ocean. Their progress apparently measured by inches.

He lunged forward, cursing the pull of the grass which hampered his stride and sapped at his energy. Strength too low for the task; the scant food failing to replace that used and, now the food was gone, hunger was turning into starvation.

"Steady!" Dumarest was at his side, a hand firm on his arm. "Take a rest."

"But—"

"Do it!" Dumarest softened his tone. "Rest now and we can keep going until twilight. Be stubborn and you'll collapse after a couple of miles." His knife flashed as he hacked free a bunch of grass. "Here, keep busy with this. Something to fill your stomach." He illustrated running a

strand between his teeth to remove the husk and pulp.
"See?"

"Can we live on it?"

"No, but it'll give you bulk and some moisture." And
give him something to do as well as taking his mind off
present difficulties. Dumarest added, "There's a run over
there. The sun's low enough to shade it and with luck we'll
get something to eat."

He moved off before Angado could comment, one hand
delving beneath his tunic to reappear with a scrap of food
concentrate wrapped in a cloth. Sweat had soaked into the
fabric, adding his own body odor to that of the ripening
wafer. Carefully he set it at the place he had noted; one
where small tunnels through the grass joined to form a
junction. Snares would have created a warning scent and an
unusual sight image and Dumarest didn't want to wait
longer than necessary. Taking up a position facing the sun,
the wind in his face, he poised the knife in his hand and
stood, waiting.

A living statue dark against the sky. Angado watched,
running strands of grass between his teeth. The gain was
small but his mouth welcomed the opportunity to chew and
swallow and the moist pulp held a refreshing tartness. More
gratifying was the opportunity to rest and he eased the ache
in back and legs, bones and muscles.

The pack was a nuisance. The need of the sacs had been
demonstrated; spread at night they collected condensed dew
and twice the fruit of an intermittent rain. But most of the
rest was useless; clothing they would never wear, empty
containers, voided ampules. . . . discarded rubbish . . . stuff
which swirled in his mind and created a sudden complexity
of dancing patterns.

Angado started, aware that he had dozed, fighting the
sleep which clogged his mind. The sun was lower than he
remembered but the dark silhouette against the sky was as
before. Then, as he watched, Dumarest exploded in a sudden blur of motion. A flash as the knife left his hand, a
darting forward, a stoop then he was upright again and
coming toward him the creature he had caught impaled on
the blade of the thrown knife.

A thing little larger than a rat, which he skinned, filled

the pelt with the guts, head and feet, then split the remainder into two segments one of which he handed to Angado.

"Eat it."

"Aren't we cooking it first?"

"There's more energy in it raw." Dumarest bit, chewed, blood rimming his mouth. "We may get something else later on."

Another rodent, a twin of the first, which Angado turned on a crude spit over the smoking fire. It was stringy and, lacking salt, flavorless, but it was hot and something to chew and a filled stomach restored his optimism.

"I could get to like this kind of life," he said, poking at the fire. "But not without a gun and a few comforts. A sleeping bag, some emergency rations, a radio to summon help if anything went wrong." The smoldering eye flared as it fed on a morsel of fat. As it died Angado said, in a different tone, "How much longer, Earl?"

"As long as it takes."

"How far, then? Damn it, you know what I mean. There has to be someone around. A settlement, a town, civilization of some kind. Even a farm. We just can't wander on forever."

The truth, but they could wander until they died, and, for Angado, that would mean the same thing.

Dumarest said, quietly, "A world's a big place. Any world. Even the residents never get to see all of it and it takes a long time for even them to spread. A planet can be settled, no riches found, the community dwindle to a string of farms. Natural increase will take care of things in time but that means a few thousand years at least. The planets which are heavily populated are old or rich or usually both."

"And, in the Burdinnion, such worlds don't exist." Angado looked at his hands. They were clenched into fists as if he wanted to fight and defeat the truth Dumarest had given him. "Krogstad," he said. "The bastard! He didn't intend for us ever to be found. He as good as killed us."

"We're alive," reminded Dumarest.

"Because of you, not him." Angado drew in his breath, fighting to master his anger. "I'll find him," he said. "If I ever get out of this I'll hunt the bastard down. And when I meet him—'' He looked again at his hands. ''We'll do it together, Earl. You've the right to be in at the kill.''

''Maybe, but I've other things to do.''

''You'll let him get away with it?'' Angado thought he understood. ''I'll do the paying. Perotto can't refuse me funds to gain revenge. He—'' He broke off, looking at Dumarest's face, remembering. ''You still think he tried to kill me?''

Dumarest said, ''That's your problem, not mine. As for the rest if I ever run into Krogstad he'll regret it. But I'm not chasing him.''

''You don't want revenge? On Lychen we'd—''

''Is Lychen a vendetta world?''

''Not exactly, but we have pride.''

''The old families,'' corrected Dumarest. ''The established clans. Only the rich can afford the type of revenge you're talking about. Only the stupid would pursue it. Families locked in strife, killing each other, using assassination, anything, just to level the score. After a while even the cause of the quarrel is forgotten but the killing goes on.''

''And pride remains.''

Dumarest said, dryly, ''Which, no doubt, is a great comfort to those who bury the dead.''

He leaned back, running strands of grass between his teeth, watching Angado's face, illuminated by the glow from the fire, harden from what it had been and not just through loss of underlying fat. The journey was forcing him to face reality; pressure accentuated by Dumarest's talk; deliberately provocative stands taken on subjects the younger man had taken for granted. A means of engaging his mind and testing his attitude. Inflexibility would have shown the man to be brittle and liable to break in an emergency. As it was the black-and-white presentations had helped to soften the monotony of the journey.

Angado said, ''Earl, those reports you heard and that flash. On the night we landed.''

''Yes?''

''I've never seen anything like them while I've been on watch. Have you?''

''No.''

"Yet we're heading toward them. Why? They could have been a natural occurrence."

"I doubt it."

"But you can't be sure."

"No." Dumarest added, "We've talked enough. Will you take the first watch or shall I?"

"I'll take it."

Angado watched as Dumarest settled then turned to look at the surrounding emptiness. The rolling plain of featureless grass now silvered by starlight into a desert of snow, of frost, of uncaring indifference. Later, when tossing in restless sleep, he dreamed of lying on it forever, his skull grinning at the skies.

The next dawn it rained and they lunged forward through wet and hampering grass. Noon brought sun and thrusting winds. Night came with hunger and tormented rest. A pattern repeated with variations over the next three days. On the fourth they reached the end of the plain.

It ended abruptly as if a giant knife had slashed the terrain from side to side in a cut which reached from left to right as far as the eye could reach. A division which proved the plain to be the summit of a plateau rearing high above the ground below. Dumarest halted well clear of the edge, one ornamented with wheeling birds, graced with the susurration of wind.

"God!" Angado, more foolhardy, had dropped to thrust his head over the edge. Turning he waved. "Look at this, Earl! Look!"

From the edge the ground fell sharply in a precipitous slope broken by rocky outcroppings, clumps of vegetation, tufts of grass and clinging vines. An almost sheer surface ending in a mass of scree far below.

"A mile!" Angado drew in his breath. "We must be a mile high at least."

Rising, Dumarest shaded his eyes and studied the terrain beyond. An expanse of raw dirt, trees, rocks, stunted bushes ran to the far horizon. Nowhere could he see signs of habitation. The edge on which he stood could run in a ragged circle and to follow it would mean being trapped on the plain. To descend would be easy and it was important they choose the right place.

He checked the compass and again looked ahead seeing nothing more than before. The instrument could be faulty or distance had compounded small, initial errors. He looked at the sky. The sun was rising and wind droned against the cliff. A blast that carried seeds and dust, leaves and debris which spun as it rode the thermals, fluttering like broken fans.

Without the compass they would have wended toward the right and, for lack of checking sightings, they must have done just that.

"Left," he said to Angado. "We'll move left and hope to find something."

They spotted it at noon, a thread of smoke, a glitter which flashed and vanished from among a clump of trees.

Angado squinted at it, puzzled, shaking his head.

"I can't make it out. There're no houses that I can see and it certainly isn't a town. The smoke must be from an open fire—but the glitter?" He grunted as it came again and quickly vanished. "The sun reflected from a window? A mirror? What?"

"Water," said Dumarest. "That's a camp of some kind. They've got a bowl of water, washing in it, maybe." He checked the direction on the compass. "That's where we'll make for."

"Sure." Angado sat down, relief had brought a sudden weakness. "All we have to do is climb down this cliff."

Dumarest examined it again, finding the surface no different from what it had been before. He checked a probable line of descent; from the edge to an outcropping to where tufts of grass could provide a series of holds, to where a narrow ledge supported a clump of tall, bamboo-like vegetation.

Opening the packs, he sorted out the clothing, the ropes he had made.

"Weave more," he told Angado. "Make them tight and strong."

He set the pace, slicing the clothing with his knife, plaiting the strands, making sure they would hold. When the rope was long enough to reach the ledge he tied it around his waist.

"Hold it fast," he warned the younger man. "If I slip ram it against the ground with your foot and throw your weight against it. Keep it tight—too much slack could jerk you over when it tightens."

"What about the other stuff?" Angado looked at the discarded litter, the sacs and painfully carried items. "You dumping it?"

"This is just a test run. Hold fast now."

Dumarest slipped over the edge, feeling dirt crumble beneath his weight, dropping until his foot hit the rocks he had spotted. More dirt plumed down over him, grit stinging his eyes. Angado's face looked anxiously through a mist of dust.

"All right, Earl?"

"Get back! Watch that rope!"

His lifeline if he should slip but Angado's death together with his own if the man was careless. Dumarest waited then resumed the descent. Grass yielded beneath his weight to reveal crusted stone traced with roots. A second tuft held and he paused to examine the face of the cliff. It was rotten, eroded with wind and weather, turning to dust beneath his touch.

He inched lower, hoping that rock would provide a firmer surface, brushing aside the tall shoots as he reached the ledge bearing the bamboo. Tall poles a couple of inches thick covered with thorned leaves which dewed the back of his left hand with blood. Behind them, hidden by the foliage, gaped the open mouth of a cave.

Suddenly it filled with vicious life.

It came with a rush, a thing gleaming with chitin, mandibles open, faceted eyes reflecting the sun as if they had been rubies. A centipede-like insect three feet long nine inches thick, multiple legs covered with cruel spines which ripped and tore at Dumarest's arm as the mandibles reached to close on his throat.

Closing on his left forearm instead as he swung it up to block the attack.

The creature doubling to drive its sting into his face.

Dumarest felt the rasp of the body as he jerked his head aside, kicking so as to drive himself out and away from the ledge. Spinning, dropping, he reached for his knife, lifting it as the insect scrabbled at his arm, the sting slamming against his shoulder. Acid stung his cheek as he stabbed upward, the blade digging deep into the armored body. A blow with little result and he freed the knife and slashed instead, the keen edge cutting deep before the sting, crippling, cutting again to lop off the last few segments of the writhing body.

Hurt, maimed, the creature twisted, raking Dumarest with mandible and spines, then reared up to catch the rope and run up it. Halting, it began to tear at the plaited strands.

"Angado!" Once weakened, the rope would break and he would fall a mile to end as a bloody pulp on the scree. "Up, man! Up!"

A shout followed by a jerk which sent Dumarest crashing hard against the face of the cliff. Above him the insect slid down the rope, the upper half of its body twisting to take a new hold, to send the entire creature scuttling down toward Dumarest's head.

A moment and it was on him, mandibles tearing at his scalp, legs ripping at his eyes. Instinct drove the knife upward to cut, slash, stab at the ruby eyes, cut away the threshing legs. Ichor oozed from the lacerated body to dew him with odorous slime. Then, as Angado hauled at the rope, the thing fell away to drop, spinning, to the ground below.

"God!" Angado dropped the rope to help Dumarest as he climbed over the edge. "Your face! What the hell happened?"

His face tightened when, later, Dumarest told him. Water from a canteen had washed away the ichor and slime and an ampule of drugs had ended the pain from the acid-burn of bites and scratches. But nothing could have saved his eyes and the lacerations on his brows told how close the sting had come.

"A thing like that living in the cliff. You were lucky, Earl. But maybe it was a loner."

"No."

"It could have been. A freak of some kind." Angado wanted to be convinced. "Or maybe they only lurk near the edge."

Dumarest said, "It had a lair behind that clump of bamboo. My guess is that we'll find others, like it wherever there is cover. Other things too—the cliff is riddled with holes and they can't all be natural. And don't forget the wind."

"What has that to do with it?"

"It blows from the ground out there to the cliff and it brings all sorts of things with it. Spores, seeds, insects, eggs, birds—anything which gets caught winds up here. Food, and where there's food there will be predators. I just happened to run into one."

Angado walked to the edge and looked over. The sun, now in its descent, threw golden light over the slope, painting it with a false warmth and gentleness.

Returning to where Dumarest sat, he said, "Aside from the insects could we climb down it?"

"With luck, maybe, but we'd need a hell of a lot of luck." Dumarest met his eyes. "With what I figure is lurking on the face it's impossible."

"So we're stuck up here."

"That's right. We're stuck—unless we can find another way down."

That night they saw lights, faint glimmers far in the distance, blooming to die as if born from a struggling fire that sputtered and fumed and roared into new and angry life.

"A camp," mused Angado. "I guess you're right, Earl. It has to be a camp."

"Maybe more than that."

"Hunters, maybe, or—" Angado blinked. "What?"

"Those reports I heard and the flash. The noises could have been sonic bangs high up and going away from us. If they had emanated at ground level we'd have run into them on the journey. The flash could have been from an Erhaft field."

"Lavender?" Angado shook his head. "A field is blue."

"Normally, yes, but the air could have colored it." Dumarest paused then added, "Or there could have been another reason. Do you know anything about generators?"

"You're talking about a malfunction in the phase effect resulting in a spectrum drop." Angado smiled with a flash of white teeth. "We studied chromatic analysis of the Erhaft field during my last semester at university. The Daley-Ash University of Space Flight," he added wryly. "I guess you could say I know something about generators."

"You surprise me."

"Why? Because I act the dilettante?" Angado shrugged. "I had an ambition when a child and tried to achieve it. I wanted to be someone who could do things. A doctor or an engineer, healing and building, even be an expert on something so I'd be respected. Family pride," he said bitterly. "A defense against family pressure. So I went to university and studied until I was told to stop wasting my time."

"So you called it a bad dream and ran from it? The necessity of having to make a decision?"

"Call it that." Angado was curt. "A family can be a prison, Earl. You live by rules not of your making. You conform to ideals established before you were born. Play along and everything's fine. Step out of line and—" His hand slapped the ground as if he were squashing an insect. "End of ambition. End of career. End of any pretense of freedom. So I sold out. Can you blame me?"

"That isn't my business. Could what I saw have been a ship?"

"It could and you know it. You've known it from the first." Hope animated the younger man's face. "That camp! If it was a ship you saw and the field was showing phase malfunction then it must have made an emergency landing. Which means—" He rose and stared at where they had seen the fire. "It's still here, Earl. Still here. A way out of this damned trap!"

"If we can get to it."

"What?" Angado slumped. "I'd forgotten. That blasted cliff. How the hell can we get down it?"

"Tell me."

"What's there to tell? We can't climb down. We can't slide or—" He broke off, shaking his head. "No. The terminal velocity would be too great. Even with air-drogues we'd never make it and that's assuming we can find material to build sledges and a slope shallow enough to try it. I must have been crazy to think about it. So what else is left?"

Dumarest said, "How about flying?"

"Hang gliders?" Angado was quick to assess the possibility. "No. It could be done but we haven't the materials. The wing would have to be strong and so would the covering. If either went we'd be dead." He frowned and said, "But maybe a kite? Two kites, big ones, one for each of us? Earl, how can we build a couple of kites?"

"From bamboo," said Dumarest. "That can be got from the ledge. I'll go down at first light and get it, it'll be safe enough now. The sacs will serve for covering and we have wire to lash things tight. Ropes, too—we'd better get on making what we need." He glanced at the sky, the stars were misted with cloud. "We want to be ready when the wind starts to blow."

The kites were box-shaped, twice the height of a man, following aerodynamic principles learned by Angado at the university. Dumarest checked the lashings, using the handle of the axe to twist them tight, the flat to test for security. The plastic sacs, opened out and cut to shape formed the major part of the covering while broad strips of various materials from the clothing provided the rest. Empty containers, voided ampules, the rubbish Angado had resented carrying—all went into the final construction. Proof of Dumarest's knowledge of the wild where even a pin was an item of inestimable value and a battered empty can an object beyond price.

"Catch hold!" He threw the end of a rope at Angado. "Pull!" He jerked his own end as the man obeyed. "Again! Once more! Good! That should do it!"

The final rope and he knotted it firmly in place before attaching it to his harness. Each checked the other and both looked grotesque with thick rolls of material bound around shins, thighs, heads, hips, arms and chest. Padding to absorb the shock of impact when they landed.

If they landed, thought Angado grimly. If the wind didn't smash them back against the cliff and the kites provided enough support to break the speed of their fall. If the ropes didn't break. The coverings rip free. The bamboo framework shatter. The scree not too hard or spiked with hidden rocks.

Doubts which didn't seem to affect Dumarest.

He said, "When the wind hits the cliff it turns up and back on itself like a cresting wave. I've been studying how grass acts in the thermals. Throw it out far enough and it doesn't come back. Once the wind catches your kite keep it heading out. If it doesn't, pull it back and try again. Got it?"

Simple instructions but not so easy to follow despite the guidelines attached to the framework. In theory the kites could be guided to a certain degree. But now, facing the acid test, Angado wasn't so sure.

He said, "Earl, I've been thinking. Maybe—"

"Now!" snapped Dumarest. "Now!" Then, as Angado hesitated, "Damn it, man! Move!"

The whip-crack of command which he obeyed, lifting the kite and running with it to the edge, muscles cracking beneath the strain. A moment of teetering then the wind took over, catching the kite, lifting it, jerking Angado off balance and off the edge of the cliff to leave him dangling in his harness.

Dumarest watched then followed, knowing the impossibility of following his instructions, knowing too they had been given for the other's benefit. The gamble was risky enough without adding an utter helplessness to the equation. Angado had been lucky, the wind which had caught him had been kind, Dumarest's wasn't so cooperative.

He grunted as the wind veered, slamming him against the cliff, the kite jerking him away again, a clinging vine trailing from his boot. He kicked free as again the wind gusted, the kite bobbing, dropping, soaring upward in a complex motion which blurred his eyes and filled his mouth with the taste of vomit. Weakness he ignored as he fought vertigo, tugging at his line to shorten the distance between himself and the kite, hanging, swaying like a pendulum beneath it as the wind roared past his ears.

The sound was too loud—he was falling too fast. He tugged at the guidelines, discarding them as the kite refused to respond. Instead he threw his body in a widening swing, forcing the kite to react to his movements. It tilted, straightened, was captured by the uprushing air. The roaring died and, suddenly, he drifted in calm.

The cliff was well to one side, a soaring wall of blotched and mottled dirt and stone. The other kite was closer to the wall and, like his own, acted as a parachute. Larger and they would have lifted their burdens but it was enough they had carried them clear and lowered them slow.

Five hundred feet above the ground one of the ropes snapped with the sound of tearing paper.

Dumarest swung, hanging on the single remaining rope, his weight pulling the kite to one side, tilting it, forcing it to lose height and lift. The roaring started again in his ears and he gripped the rope, climbing up it, catching the inner structure of the kite and hanging from it as the ground rushed up toward him. A moment of strain with the force of the wind fighting against his arms, muscles burning, cracking with the effort to hold on, then a sidewise swoop and the sudden jarring rasp as the kite slammed against the wall of the cliff.

A glancing blow, repeated, the third time shattering the structure and leaving nothing but a mass of splintered bamboo, shreds of plastic, wire, frayed and disintegrating rope.

From it Dumarest rolled, falling through a clump of bushes, over thickly tufted grass, to half-fall, half-slide over the fan of scree. To come to rest in a cloud of dirt among a scatter of stones.

"Earl!" Angado came running. He had landed safely and close. Now he knelt, turning Dumarest over, the anxiety on his face turning to relief as he sat upright. "Are you hurt?"

"I don't think so." There was no blood, no ache of broken bones, just numbness and the promise of bruises. The padding had done its job. "You?"

"Fine."

Dumarest nodded and climbed to his feet. The padding made movement awkward and he cut it away, leaving the scraps where they had fallen. Stretching, he took cautious strides. Luck and experience had been with him. One had thrown him into the bushes the other had made him fall like a baby or a drunk, not fighting gravity, yielding to it instead, muscles lax and supple.

"We made it!" Angado drew in his breath as he stared at the towering wall of the cliff. "By God, we made it! All we have to do now is get to the ship. Which way do we head, Earl?"

Dumarest looked at his wrist compass, the face broken, the dial twisted, the interior useless.

Chapter Five

Brother Dexter straightened from the fire feeling the nagging twinge in his back grow to a sudden fire, one accompanied by a moment of giddiness so that he stood immobile in the smoke now rising from the coals. The effects of age as he knew, familiar but now growing more frequent. Soon he would have to yield his place to a younger man and be content with simple, routine duties, but not just yet. Not when there was still so much to be done.

The sin of pride; his lips quirked as he recognized it. The justification for hanging on and, by so doing, denying others the opportunity to fulfill themselves. They could do the work as well as he and probably far better. Lloyd, Kollar, Boyle, Pollard, Galpin—any of a host of others—they had been chosen for this mission and he had insisted on being its head. But now, feeling his age, he wished he hadn't been so importunate.

The pains eased a little and he stepped back from the fire. A tall, gaunt figure, bare feet thrust into plain sandals, his body wrapped in a cowled robe of brown homespun, the fabric held by a cord belting the waist. The garb of all monks of the Church of Universal Brotherhood. Sometimes called the Universal Church. Sometimes just the Church. The name was unimportant only the work they did. The work and the creed they preached and carried to wherever men were to be found. The simple doctrine that no man is an island. All belonged to the *corpus humanitatis*. That if each could look at the other and remember that *there, but for the grace of God, go I* the millenium would have arrived.

He would never see it. No monk now alive would ever do

that. Men bred too fast and traveled too far but it was something to live for. A purpose to his existence.

One which now could be near its end.

"Brother!" Lloyd came toward him, face anxious, the stubbled skull framed by his thrown-back cowl. "I saw you stagger," he said. "For a moment I thought you would collapse."

"A momentary dizziness caused by the smoke." A possibility and so not wholly a lie. And to increase the other's concern would not be kind. "The others?"

"At their duties. Brother Kollar is with Sadoria."

"Any improvement?"

"None." Lloyd hesitated, scraping at the dirt with a sandal. "Kollar thinks he will die."

And, with the engineer, would go their only hope of repairing the *Guilia*. Dexter looked at the ship where it had come to rest. A good landing; Ryder, though a hard captain, knew his job, but even though the vessel appeared undamaged its heart was dead. The generator which alone could free them from the prison they were in.

Dexter added more damp leaves to the fire, stubborn in his refusal to yield to incapacity. The smoke plumed thicker, rising in a twisting column to be caught by the higher winds which shredded it and carried it toward the soaring wall of the escarpment. A cliff which alone would be an attraction for tourists if ever it could be tamed. If Velor could be tamed with it. But even if both were done, tourists were few in the Burdinnion and the chance of rescue was remote.

Negative thoughts which dulled the day and Dexter turned from the fire, his face resolute. If they could do nothing else the monks must radiate a calm serenity and the conviction that all would be well. A duty owed to the captain, the crew, the other passengers the *Guilia* had carried. A hard bunch but each had their inner secrets, their private fears. All the need for consolation. To provide it the monks had set up their portable church manned now by Boyle.

Before him, through the mesh dividing the booth, he could see the taut, strained face, the eyes wild, the brow dewed with sweat. Sforza Bux, small in more ways than one, now trembling with emotion as he eased his soul.

The litany of sin was all too familiar; an outpouring limited

by the capabilities of the human condition, but magnified by
an uneasy conscience.

". . . cheated, Brother. I looked at the bottom card and
knew Ranevsky couldn't have held four aces so I upped the
stake and forced him to call. But I shouldn't have won and
shouldn't have taken the money because it was wrong to
cheat. And I found some berries yesterday which I didn't turn
in. I ate them instead and that was cheating too of a kind. I
wasn't even hungry."

A man wanting to be clean and decent but trapped in the
conditioning imposed by his environment. Wanting to rid
himself of guilt and make a clean start and doomed to fail no
matter how often he tried. But he tried—that was the important thing. And, trying, yielded himself to the power of the
Church.

"Cheating is a sin," said Boyle. "It is tantamount to lying
and a partner to theft. It is dishonest and unworthy and
lessens those who yield to it. In the situation we are in it is
even more heinous for unless we have mutual trust we are
less than beasts. Think now of the sins you have done. Assess
them in your mind. Void them with words of requital."

After a moment Boyle threw a switch.

"Look into the light of forgiveness," he said gently. "Bathe
in the flame of righteousness and be cleansed of all pain, all
sin. Yield to the benediction of the Universal Brotherhood."

The pale face of Sforza Bux shone with reflected color as
he stared into the benediction light. A swirling kaleidoscope
of shifting hues which gave his features an ethereal quality.
The light was hypnotic, the subject subservient, the monk a
trained master of his craft. Under his suggestion the suppliant
relaxed to slip into a deeper trance. One in which he under-
went a stringent penance; time encapsulated to provide a
subjective torment of being robbed, cheated, denied and yet
accepting all to find a final absolution.

Later he would be given the bread of forgiveness and, if on
too many worlds too many suppliants came to kneel before
the benediction light for the sake of the food alone, it was a
fair exchange. For all who so knelt were conditioned against
the act of murder.

*   *   *

Captain Ryder was short, square, his face creased with a mesh of lines, the pattern marred by a deep scar running over one cheek. Surgery could have removed it but he retained it for the bonus it gave to his appearance. Dealing with the scum he met in the Burdinnion every little bit helped.

Now he scowled at the two men standing before him. Both looked like hell, clothing worn, chafed, showing rents. Faces almost identical in their marks of privation. But, instinctively, he sensed the elder of the two was the leader.

To Dumarest he snapped, "How the hell did you get here?"

"We followed your smoke."

"I don't mean that. We registered no ship since we landed. That's over two weeks ago—closer to three. If you had a camp why didn't you answer our beacon?"

Dumarest said, "What good would it have done? Would you have come for us?"

"No—but you could have come to us. Your ship—" Ryder broke off then said, questioningly, "You do have a ship?"

"No."

"Then what the hell are you doing here?"

"We're all that's left of a survey team," said Dumarest quickly. "Five of us were dropped on the plateau together with equipment and supplies for six months. That was a month ago. The Tziak-Wenko Consortium. You may know of them."

Ryder frowned and shook his head.

"Based on Chalowe," said Dumarest. "A new and ambitious outfit. They send out teams to make a survey and then figure if it's worth developing the area. We picked this dump." He spat in the dirt. "For me you can keep it."

"Trouble?"

"Three days after landing. A storm first then we got hit by predators. They killed two and hurt the other so bad he only lasted three days. The radio was smashed, the supplies spoiled and scattered, we were lucky to stay alive. Then we saw you land and headed toward where we figured you'd be." Dumarest held up his wrist and displayed the ruined compass. "If you hadn't made smoke we'd never have found you."

"That was the monks." Ryder jerked his head to where

they stood before the church. "God knows why they bother. There's no one around to see it. I guess they hope to keep up morale. Six months, you say?"

"That's right."

"So your ship won't be back for another five."

"At least. That's why we'd like to take passage with you. How bad is the damage?" Dumarest added, "We saw you land and spotted the color of your field. Phase malfunction, right? How long will it take your engineer to effect repairs?"

Ryder said, curtly, "Why don't you ask him yourself?"

Sadoria lay in his cabin, a place ornamented with illustrations in vivid color depicting an age-old act in countless variations. Obscenity somehow enhanced by the presence of the monk who sat at the side of the cot. Like all monks, Brother Kollar had trained in basic medicine but he had pursued his studies further than most. Under his hands the writhing figure of the engineer eased a little but his droning babble never ceased.

"Traumatic shock induced by drug abuse," explained the monk. "In a sense his brain has been short-circuited and the censor divorced from the speech center. At this moment he is lost in a world of violent hallucinations and, inevitably, his psychosomatic reactions will result in a total degeneration of all faculties." His hands moved a little, touching the throat, the nerves of the neck. "I am trying to induce a somnolent period so as to give him hypnotic therapy."

"Will it cure him?"

"No, but it will help his pain." The monk met Dumarest's eyes. "It's all I can do, brother."

Outside the cabin Angado halted in the passage and shook his head. "That poor devil! If ever that happens to me—"

"Forget him." Dumarest was impatient. "I want the truth now. Can you repair this ship?"

"I could try."

"Anyone can do that. Can you repair it?"

"I'd have to examine the generator first. I guess the captain would give permission for that."

"We'll find out. Let me handle it. Just don't volunteer information. If I ask a question you signal an answer; one blink for yes, two for no. Got it?"

"Yes, but—"

"When this ship leaves we have to be on it. Making a deal may not be easy. If the captain ever finds out we were dumped and why it'll be impossible." Dumarest glanced along the passage. "Get to the engine room. I'll meet you there with Ryder."

He was in the control room with his navigator and the steward. They, together with the engineer, formed the entire complement of the *Guilia*. Normal for the kind of vessel it was; a free-trader with each crew member sharing in the profits and all doing a double stint for the sake of a larger cut. The engine room reflected Sadoria's personality, a place thick with grime and plastered with lurid pictures. Only the generator looked clean.

Ryder frowned as he saw Angado kneeling beside it. He'd already removed one cover and was at work on a second.

Dumarest said, watching his eyes, "How does it look so far? Bad? I thought it might be. Can you do anything with it? Good." He looked at the captain. "Do you want us to go ahead or would you rather wait for rescue?"

A loaded question. The radio beacon signaling the position of the vessel and calling for help emitted a wide-range broadcast but one now dampened and blocked by the bulk of the planet. Even if picked up there was no certainty of response. Rescue was determined by the possibility of recompense and, if too much trouble, was rarely attempted.

Ryder said, "If you can repair it go ahead."

"And?"

"We'll talk about that when it's done."

"Before it's done," said Dumarest. "Passage for the both of us to your next world of landing and—"

"When it's done!" snarled Ryder. "What's the good of haggling over something until we've got it?"

He stormed away, a man living on his nerves, one too close to bankruptcy to have the patience to argue. Rescue would ruin him but without it he was stuck on a hostile world. Dumarest was his only chance but he hated to admit it.

"He'll pay." Angado looked up from the generator. "He'll have no choice."

"There's always a choice," said Dumarest. "Promises can be broken and a fee given can always be taken back. But if I press him hard then ease off he'll be too grateful to hold a grudge. He'll give us passage and what he can afford. It won't be much but he won't resent giving it." He looked at the exposed interior of the generator. The components seemed undamaged but one unit showed a shimmering rainbow effect where it faced the others. "Is that it?"

"If I said it wasn't?"

"You'd be a liar. Phase malfunction is confined to the similarity units. A burn-out would have left a deposit. An overload the same but in a different sector."

"And power-pulse feedback?"

"The regulator takes care of that."

"And if it doesn't?" Angado didn't wait for an answer. "You're dead, that's what. Or drifting. You know a lot about generators, Earl. Where did you study?"

On ships and helped by a man long dead. Dumarest saw his face pictured on the shining surface of the generator units, multiplied by conduits, flat planes, distorted by convex swellings. The face of the captain of the first ship he had ever seen. One in which he had stowed away to be found, threatened with eviction, saved by an old man's kindly whim.

"Earl?"

"It doesn't matter." Dumarest squeezed shut his eyes and shook his head to clear it of fogging memories. "How long will you be?"

"As long as it takes." Angado smiled as he gave a remembered answer to the question. "As you told me on the plain."

"Days? Weeks?"

"It's a matter of synchronization. That and balance of similarity. Nine nines is as good as we're ever going to get and we can't reach that without specialized equipment, which isn't here. Seven nines is good. Five nines is the least we can get away with. I'll have to use a mirror-reflection phaseometer and I'll need help to compute the trial-and-error readings. The first I can rig from what's available. The second?"

"I can manage that."

"Good," said Angado. "Let's get to it."

It had been raining and the streets of Anfisa held an unaccustomed shine. A gleam in which the drooping pennants showed like smeared patches of oily hues and the rounded domes with their spike ornamentations were reflected in a profusion of altered shapes so that the town seemed to be haunted by bizarre creatures of some undersea forest.

An association Avro didn't make as he stood at the window looking toward the distant field, the spot where his ship was resting. Where it had rested for days now after a journey in which three of the crew had died and two others had suffered irreparable damage to hearts and kidneys.

That sacrifice had been unnecessary and stood as a silent accusation.

What had gone wrong?

The *Thorn* was behind schedule and no message had been received to give the reason. Accident? Damage? A burst engine causing the vessel to drift helplessly in space between the stars?

Madness?

The possibilities were endless and to speculate a waste of mental energy. It was time to search out facts and to be more determined than before. The factor could have been careless or hiding the truth for reasons of his own. The *Thorn*, on a regular route, would have gained friends and backers who needed to protect their investment.

Avro saw a touch of scarlet in the street below. The flash of color vanishing as it was spotted. Minutes later Byrne knocked and entered the chamber.

"Master!" The acolyte bowed. "I have—"

"News? What of the *Thorn*?"

Impatience displayed with an interruption; behavior so alien to normal procedure as to cause the acolyte to stand mute. A silent reproof Avro recognized as he knew the reason. Time had been wasted—Byrne could have been about to tell him what he had demanded to know. The interruption was a blatant display of inefficient conduct.

He said evenly, "You may report."

"Yes, Master." This time there was no bow. "I have gathered all available information from the field as you ordered. Nothing new has been gained but Cyber Ishaq arrived on the *Panoyan* as I was questioning Amontabo, the Hausi agent. Cyber Ishaq waits outside."

He was too young, too ambitious, too eager to make his mark. Avro studied him as he walked forward to make his greeting, the bow almost perfunctory as if he resented the older man's superior rank. Yet, superficially, he was deferential.

"I was ordered to report to you and place myself at your disposal," he said. "It meant terminating my association with the Matriarch of Lunt. However, as I assured her, a replacement will be provided. I understand you are here to meet the *Thorn.*"

"That is so." The information would have been relayed to Ishaq from Central Intelligence—but why hadn't he been told of the man's coming? Avro added, "The ship is behind schedule. No reason has yet been given to account for the delay."

"I can provide it. The vessel is under quarantine."

"Quarantine?"

"It is now in closed orbit around this planet." If Ishaq took a mental delight in displaying his superior knowledge he didn't show it. "The information has been kept secret for obvious reasons. The suspicion of plague would create a panic and affect the financial welfare of this world."

"How do you know this?"

"A radio message was picked up by one of our monitoring stations. A monk of the Church, Brother Jofre, was informing his superior of an incident that happened during flight. A sudden illness followed by the forced abandonment of two passengers. The superior must have informed the appropriate authorities." Ishaq paused then added, "It was something they dared not ignore."

The Church had friends in high places and the Cyclan had long known of the net of communication built on the super-radios incorporated into every benediction light. A system not to be compared to the efficient working of Central Intelligence but good enough for the activities of the monks.

Why had Jofre radioed ahead?

Had it been an act of revenge against Krogstad for his high-handed action or a genuine concern for the people of Anfisa? A question now without relevance; the *Thorn* was in quarantine. The ship and all it held isolated and beyond reach.

Avro said, "The passengers who were evicted. Was Dumarest one of them?"

"That has not been determined. Nor has his presence on the vessel."

"You doubt the probability?"

"The fact. It has yet to be verified."

The truth as Avro knew; no probability could be regarded as certain and his own convictions were not enough. If Dumarest was on the *Thorn* he was safely held. The ship was now a prison. But if he hadn't been on it or was no longer on it—what then?

Wait?

If Dumarest was free then delay increased the risk of losing him. Yet to contact the *Thorn* direct would be to reveal an interest it was better to keep hidden.

Amontabo solved the problem.

The Hausi was thick-set, strongly built, his dark cheeks slashed with the livid scars which were the castemark of his Guild. A man who never lied, but that was not to say he always told all of the truth. A dealer, go-between, agent, proxy—the Hausi performed a variety of needed roles. And Amontabo knew of the power of the Cyclan.

He bowed as he entered the chamber, first to Avro then to Ishaq. No accident, he had taken the trouble to discover who was senior. His words, when he spoke, were carefully aimed between the two.

"My lords, it has been an honor to have served you. I only trust the information I was able to gain will be of value. Of course, there were difficulties, a matter of certain arrangements which had to be made—closed beam radio with double scrambler is not something used every day."

"You will be paid," said Ishaq.

Avro, more discerning, said, "All expenses will be met as promised together with the agreed fee. In addition certain advantages will come your way." Commissions, fees, advantages, opportunities to partake of certain profits—the Cyclan could be generous when it chose. "Your report?"

"Negative, my lord. Dumarest is not on the *Thorn*."

"Are you positive?"

"Captain Krogstad listed each and every member of his crew together with all passengers. Most of the passengers and all of the crew are known. Of the rest none fits the description you provided. The man you are interested in is not on the ship."

Ishaq said, "Was he ever?"

Amontabo shrugged, shoulders lifting, hands rising, palms upward in a gesture which was an answer in itself.

"Assuming the man was on the ship and is not there now the conclusion is that he must be one of the two men dumped on that planet," said Avro. "What is its name?"

"Velor, my lord." The Hausi added, "A harsh and barren world."

"There is no need to elaborate. Concentrate on the men. What is known about them?"

"One, younger than the man for whom you are looking, is known to the gambler who has seen him before. His name is Angado Nossak and he was the one who fell sick. The other could have been a mercenary or a miner. Five people swear to that impression."

"His name?"

"Earl, my lord. The younger man was heard to call him that and he was so registered."

Earl! Earl Dumarest! Avro felt the mind-opening euphoria of the proof of his prediction. He had been right. The quarry he hunted had been exactly where he had said it would be.

Ishaq said, "There is no doubt?"

"None, my lord. Krogstad uses a lie-detector as a check against possible trouble. Most vessels in the Burdinnion follow the practice. With worlds so close and markets available the temptation to steal a ship is high."

And so the precaution, the risk Dumarest had been forced to take. A small one; who would be looking for him so far from Baatz? Who would have questioned the sworn testimony of his death?

The answer was reflected in the window Avro faced; his own shape limned against the darkening sky. An unanswerable demonstration of his efficiency; if it hadn't been for Krogstad's action Dumarest would have been taken and on his way to interrogation.

And now?

Avro knew the answer to that too—the hunt must go on.

Chapter Six

The generator was stubborn. Stripped, cleaned, reassembled, it held the beauty of functional design but remained inert. Before the Erhaft field could be created to swathe the *Guilia* in its blue cocoon and let it traverse the void at a velocity far greater than that of light the similarity components had to be aligned to near perfection. Not true perfection, that was impossible, but 99.9999999 percent of perfection, the nine nines which was the aim and dream of every engineer.

Angado didn't even try to get it. Instead he aimed for the lowest workable alignment of five nines. It took a week to achieve it. Another two before the *Guilia* completed its journey to Yuanka.

They landed in a storm of wind and dust; minute grains of sand and dirt which eddied like a fog and settled in a gray coating over the town, the field, the warehouses along the perimeter. Within seconds the *Guilia* was a copy of the other vessels standing on the dirt, a gray ghost standing like a shadow among the roiling dunes, detail lost in the diffused sunlight of a dying day.

Ryder was blunt. "You're fools to stop here," he said to them both. "Stay with the ship. I can use a good engineer, a handler too." His eyes moved toward Dumarest. "And from what I've seen you'd make a good assistant to your friend."

"Thanks for the offer," said Dumarest. "But no thanks."

"You?" Ryder grunted as Angado shook his head. "Well, I guess you know your own business, but take some advice. Watch yourselves—Yuanka is a bad world on which to be stranded. If you are then mention me to a few of the captains.

64

Some of them know me. All of them could use a good engineer."

"We'll remember that," said Dumarest. "And thanks again." He held out his hand. "The rest of the fee, Captain? We'd like to leave with the monks."

They alone were disembarking, loaded with bales, bundles, assorted supplies. Brother Dexter smiled his appreciation when Dumarest offered to help, frowned when he added a stipulation.

"Robes? You both want robes?"

"Just the loan of a couple," said Dumarest. Then added, as explanation, "For protection against the wind. Also it'll be easier to wear them than carry them."

And, robed, they would merge among the monks, becoming members of the party. A thing Dexter realized even as he nodded to Pollard to supply the garments. Normally he would have refused the request; the Church took no part in deception practiced by others, but neither did it refuse needed help. And here, on Yuanka, the Church needed all the help it could get.

The wind caught them as they trudged from the ship, dumping their goods and leaving monks to guard them as they went back for more. Three trips and they rested, faces grayed by the dust, eyes stinging, nostrils blocked. As they waited, backs to the wind, the *Guilia* headed again into space, spurning the dust and dirt of the planet for the clean emptiness between the stars.

"Ryder's a fool." Angado shouted over the wind. "That generator's shot and needs replacing. He didn't even wait to hire another engineer."

A replacement for Sadoria now lying in a shallow grave on Velor.

Dumarest said, "He knows what he's doing."

"Like hell he does. He didn't even wait for passengers or cargo."

An assumption which displayed Angado's ignorance of free-trader operations. Ryder was impatient but neither crazy nor a fool. He would have contacted the field-agent by radio, have learned there were no passengers or cargo bound for his next world of call, and have decided not to waste time. A gambler risking that the generator would hold and that he could get profitable commissions if he beat other vessels.

Things Dumarest didn't bother to explain; the problem at hand was enough.

To Dexter he said, "Where is this stuff to be taken? Where is the church?"

"We have it with us." Brother Dexter gestured at the bales. "We have none established here on Yuanka as yet but the authorities have given us permission to stay."

"And build?"

"Yes. Beyond the field. In sector nine." The monk pointed to where the wind fluttered a tangle of pennants; strips and fragments of cloth and plastic adorning a sleezy collection of hovels. "Over there, I think. In Lowtown."

On every world they were the same; the repositories of the stranded, the deprived, the desperate. Dumping grounds for the unwanted and differing only in the degree of filth, stench and squalor they displayed. Shacks made of rubbish; mounds of dirt roofed with discarded sheets of plastic, hammered tin, cartons, the remains of packing cases. Huts fashioned of any scrap material to hand. The home of vice and crime, of degeneracy and poverty.

The monks' new home.

Brother Dexter set to work as soon as the wind eased and by the time it had died the church had taken shape. A tent firmly held by stakes, ropes and pegs. One containing space for a communal kitchen, a dispensary, accommodation for the monks and the all-important cubicle containing the benediction light. The portable church now incorporated into the main structure but with its entrance outside. Even before it was finished the line had begun to form.

"Patience." Brother Galpin, young, trying hard to practice the virtue he preached, held up an admonishing hand. "Give us time to get established."

"You have food?" The woman was in her thirties and looked twice as old. A shawl was draped over rounded shoulders and hugged to her hollow chest. "Please, Brother, you have food?"

"And medicine?" Another woman, almost a twin of the first, thrust forward, her face anxious. "My man is sick, dying, medicine could save him. You have medicine?"

"Some. Antibiotics and—"

"You will dispense it?" The woman's voice rose with

kindled hope. "Give it free? We can't pay and my man is dying!"

"And my child!"

"My brother and . . ."

"Food! I'm too weak to work!"

"Give me . . . Give . . . Give . . ."

Brother Galpin retreated from the sudden clamor, the outstretched hands and avid faces. A man beyond his depth and almost overwhelmed. He hit one of the ropes holding the tent, tripped and would have fallen if Dumarest hadn't caught his arm.

"Back!" He confronted the mob, face framed by the thrown-back cowl of his borrowed robe, blazed with a harsh determination. "Back, all of you! Get about your business!"

"But, Brother—"

"Come back tomorrow." Dumarest glared at the speaker, a thin runt of a man with a face like a weasel. "If you want to stay you can work. Grab a shovel and start clearing away this grit. We need a trench running over there. A wall built just here. Who will volunteer?"

"I'd help but I'm sick." The weasel-faced man coughed and spat blood. "See? My lungs are gone. The mines did that. I need medicine or I'll die."

"And me! I need it more than him. He's lying, anyway, that blood came from a bitten cheek." Another man, stocky, his face bitter, thrust the other to one side. "Help those who need it most, Brother. My wife is dying. You can save her."

"Maybe." Dumarest looked at him. "Name?"

"Worsley. Carl Worsley. You want help I'll arrange it. But my wife—"

"Get the help," said Dumarest. "The quicker we get settled the sooner we can start helping." He added, "But your wife needn't wait. Bring her as soon as you can."

She was thin, emaciated, with huge, luminous eyes. Her hair, once rich and dark with the sheen of natural oil, hung dull and lank over bony shoulders and shriveled breasts. Her cheeks, hollow, held the flush of fever and when she breathed her chest echoed to a liquid gurgling.

Looking at Dumarest, Brother Kollar shook his head.

"No!" Worsley had seen the gesture. "No, she can't be beyond help! Dear God, no!"

"I'm sorry." Kollar had seen such scenes too often but always he felt the pain as much as those more personally involved. "The tissue degeneration is too far advanced for anything we can do. I can ease her pain and give her hypnotic conditioning but—"

"What's that?"

Dumarest said, "She will be in a subjective world in which there will be no pain, no fear. Suggestion will give her as much happiness as she could hope for and the trance will last until she no longer needs it."

"Until she dies, you mean?" Worsley clenched his fists as Dumarest nodded. "You thinking of passing her out?"

"No, but if she was my wife I wouldn't hesitate."

"You? A monk? Why, you bastard I—"

"I'm not a monk," said Dumarest sharply. "And watch your mouth. You came here begging, remember. Pleading for what help could be given. Well, that's it. All of it. Did you hope for a miracle?"

"I . . ." Worsley swallowed, his eyes filling with moisture. "I thought, I'd hoped—God! Dear God don't let her die!"

A useless prayer and he knew it. Surgery could save the woman; cryogenic storage while new lungs were grown from fragments of her own tissue. Her body laved with selected antibiotics, strengthened with intravenous feeding, bolstered with supportive mechanisms. A long and tedious process even with the aid of slow time but she would live.

All it took was money.

Money Worsley didn't have. What no one in any Lowtown had. The stench which filled the air was the reek of abject poverty.

The dust storms were intermittent and happened only when strong winds blew from the northeast after a dry period. The grit they carried was abrasive, fretting the thin coverings and opening roofs to the sky. Even as the church was being constructed men were busy patching their hovels.

Watching them Angado said, "They remind me of bees. Always working, never still, yet what they do can be wiped out in a single day. As a hive is robbed of the honey it may have taken months to store. Yet they go on doing the same old thing again and again." He glanced at the church. "Like our friends the monks. Preaching, giving aid, comfort, food when they have it. And for what?''

"Do they need a reason?''

"They claim to have one.''

"A goal,'' said Dumarest. "They want to change the way men behave. Those who preach peace have always wanted that. And, always, they have failed.''

As the monks on Yuanka would fail. As they would on all bleak and hostile worlds. Jungles in which to be tolerant was to be dead.

Dumarest narrowed his eyes as he studied the men Worsley had gathered. Volunteers all, but some had subtle differences from the majority. They worked but accomplished little and seemed too interested in the area leading toward the heart of Lowtown. Watching for something, he guessed, or waiting for someone. He had a good idea of whom it might be.

"It looks good.'' Angado nodded toward the church. "Big and clean and it stands out a mile. A nice position too, it can be seen both from the field and the town. Brother Dexter knows his stuff. I'll bet this isn't the first time he's set up a church. Brother Lloyd was telling me something about him. Old, stubborn, but clever.''

A man shrewd enough to have selected the best spot available and surely he must know what could well happen? Dumarest turned as the monk came toward them. Dexter was genial but firm.

"It is time you returned your borrowed robes,'' he said. "Brother Kollar reported the incident in the infirmary. I do not blame you but your attitude is not ours. A suppliant could have gained the impression that we terminate the lives of the sick placed in our care.''

"I told Worsley I wasn't a monk.''

"He may not have believed you.''

"It may be as well for you if others don't either.'' Dumarest glanced at the men who seemed to be waiting. "There could be those who don't welcome your presence here. They might hesitate to object if they think you stronger than you are.''

"Eight instead of six.'' Dexter shook his head. "You mean well but I must insist. Our foundation here must not rest on deception. Your robe, please.'' The old monk turned to Angado who had stood quietly by, listening. "And yours also. We are on this world by sufferance of the authorities and dare not risk the possibility of a misunderstanding. You both lack the training necessary to follow the philosophy of the Church.''

"Peace," said Dumarest. "But that's something you have to fight for."

"To achieve," corrected the monk. "The robes?"

"Are they really that important?"

"The garments, no, what virtue lies in a piece of cloth? But as a symbol of what we are and are trying to accomplish—"

"The credo," Dumarest met the old monk's eyes. "There," he said softly, "but for the grace of God, go I. The thing you want all to remember; the rich, the whole, the comfortable when they look at the sick, the poor, the deprived. But it works both ways and, at times, you could forget that. The sick and maimed and hopeless you feel so concerned about look at the spoiled and pampered, the strong, the ruthless. They can see the benefits of being cruel and arrogant, and they too could think that there, but for the grace of God, they could be. And they might want to alter things a little. Correct the balance in their favor. Could you blame them if they tried?"

"The Church can never condone violence."

"Just accept it and preach that others should do the same? To be meek? To believe that to bend the head is to avoid the kick in the rear? How much punishment do you expect people to take?"

"There are worlds even now where criminals are maimed as a punishment for their crimes," said Dexter. "Once such things were common but now are rare. Soon that barbarism will vanish. As will other things." He held out his hand. "The robes, please. A monk, above all, must practice humility."

Angado watched as the monk moved away, the robes over his arm. Beneath his own he had worn clothing similar to Dumarest's, a knife thrust into his boot, the axe dumped with them riding in his belt.

He said, "You were hard on him, Earl. Why? Dexter does his best and isn't a bad man."

"He's too good for this world." Dumarest gestured at the huddle comprising Lowtown. "And for any other like it.

He's a fool. He's done his stint in the past and should now be taking things easy."

"Monks never do that."

"They should."

"They can't. That's what dedication is all about. It was unfair you talking to him the way you did. Brother Dexter's not stupid, he knows human nature as well as anyone, but he has to keep doing what he believes in." Angado paused then added, "As you would in his position. But then I suppose you'd run classes in unarmed combat and teach suppliants to use a knife. All in the name of peace."

"No," said Dumarest. "Survival."

"Kill or be killed." Angado shook his head. "God, but you're hard. People don't live like that, not even in this slum. They share a common misfortune and make the best of it. Brother Dexter and the other monks know that. That's why they're so against violence. Once it starts who knows where it will end?"

Dumarest shrugged, not answering. He looked at the sky then to where a knot of men had gathered to the far side of the church. Among them he noticed those he had spotted earlier. All looked toward the heart of Lowtown.

To Angado he said, "Find Worsley and bring him to me."

"Why do you—"

"Do it! And don't get involved no matter what happens. Remember that, don't get involved."

"Trouble?" The younger man looked around. The monks had gathered in front of the church, Dexter still holding the reclaimed robes. "I can't see anything."

"It hasn't happened yet. Well, I tried to warn him but he wouldn't listen."

"Who?"

"Brother Dexter," said Dumarest. "He's due a visitor."

He came as such men always did, confident, smiling, enjoying the moment, the pleasure to come. A man middle-aged, middle-sized, his face bland, his clothing good and clean but not too obviously expensive. Heavy rings glinted on his fingers and his hair, thick and dark, framed prominent cheekbones and deep-set eyes.

He wasn't alone. At his side trotted a smaller version of

himself, thinner, older, the sharply pointed nose and darting eyes betraying the questing, curious nature of the man. Two others, big, stocky, followed at the rear. Both carried staves a yard long and, Dumarest guessed, loaded with lead.

Worsley said, "That's Gengiz. The small one is Birkut. He keeps the accounts and tallies the score. The two big ones are his bodyguard."

"The take?"

"A zobar a person a week."

"How much is a zobar?"

"The price of half a day's work at the field—if you can get it."

"And if you don't pay?"

"You know the answer to that."

"I know," said Dumarest. "But he doesn't." He gestured toward Angado. "Tell him."

"You pay or your shack gets ruined. Your things get stolen. Your food spoiled. After that you start getting hurt." Worsley was bitter. "He calls it insurance. He'll even lend you the premiums but, after a while, if you still don't or can't pay, he collects."

"Nice," said Dumarest. "Just think of all the good things that money would have provided. Your wife's sick—she would have liked the soup and drugs you didn't get because you avoided trouble and paid."

"I paid," said Worsley tightly. "But I didn't like it. And you're wrong about one thing, mister. My wife isn't sick—she's dead. And to hell with you!"

He strode away and Dumarest looked at his companion.

"You see?"

"See what? I—"

"The reality of that garbage you were spouting. The rubbish about people sharing a common misfortune and making the best of it. You live in a jungle and you'd better realize it. You can't stop violence. All life is a continual act of violence. In order to survive you have to fight every step of the way and keep on fighting. Against disease, starvation, thirst, heat, cold, nakedness. Against the parasites wanting to feed off you. Lice and insects and ordinary predators. And against scum like Gengiz."

"He should be stopped."

"Maybe, but not by you. It's none of your business."

"But—"

"Forget it."

Dumarest held a broom, a pole tipped with a wide fan of bristles, and he used it as he followed Angado as the man moved toward the group of monks. Curious, he wanted to hear what was being said. Dumarest had already guessed.

"So you see, brothers, what the position is." Gengiz had made the preliminary spiel, his voice soft, devoid of threat, almost gentle as he urged cooperation. "In order to maintain the peace we must abide by the rules and as Mayor it is my duty to see that everyone complies. As intelligent men you can see that. As you can see that to patrol the area requires men who have to be paid. A form of tax per head of the population takes care of that. It is small, a zobar a head a week, but in your case—well, perhaps we could discuss it in private?"

Dexter shook his head. "That will not be necessary."

"It would be best."

"No. We have permission to establish our church here. That permission was granted by the authorities. The tax you mention is unlawful."

Gengiz said, softly, "Brother, answer me one thing—have you ever been in this situation before?"

"Many times."

"And must have learned from your experience. Now, if we could go somewhere to be alone?"

Seclusion where the mask could be dropped and the naked threat revealed. Pay or suffer. The structure of the church damaged, monks beaten up, suppliants threatened, stores and supplies ruined or stolen. Even a demonstration could be given—a broken arm or shattered kneecap a hint of what was to come if refusal continued.

Things Dexter knew, as he realized that to yield was to destroy the aim of the Church. To bow to the threat of violence was to condone it. To pay the levy Gengiz demanded was to buy peace at too high a price—yet to refuse was to invite harsh retribution.

Dexter looked at the sun, the sky, aware of the monks at his back, of the watching faces all around. The moment of truth he had known so often before; the hardest thing for any

monk to take. Those who served the Church could not be
weak in either spirit or body yet that strength had to be
sublimated to the greater ideal. To be meek. To be humble.
To trust that, by example, they would give rise to a protective
concern.

"Well?" Gengiz was becoming impatient. "Have you nowhere we could be alone?"

"There is nothing to decide. Therefore no good purpose
would be served by further conversation."

"I see. Birkut!"

The small man stepped forward as Gengiz and his bodyguard moved away. A toady, basking in the reflection of the
other's power, as poisonous as a serpent. His voice held an
oily note of subtle menace.

"The Mayor is being kind," he said. "He understands
your problems and is eager to accommodate you. Think it
over. Discuss it with the others. It could end as a matter of a
percentage—a share of donations." His smirk was as oily as
his tone. "You have until sunset."

Chapter Seven

Yuanka's sun was a sullen ball of smoldering ochre edged by a flickering corona of orange. Colors which combined with the murk in the atmosphere to produce a purple haze as sunset drew near. In it the perimeter fence surrounding the field showed as a misty web topped by lamps which, later, would illuminate the mesh with a vivid glow.

The fence encompassing Lowtown was less obvious but just as restricting. Dumarest looked at the cleared strip encircling the area, the deep ditch dug beyond it, the huts set at strategic points. Those controlling the planet had taken precautions against the danger residing in the hungry and desperate.

"Nice." Angado had accompanied Dumarest. "Try to break out and they'll gun down anyone reaching the ditch. I'll even bet they've got a curfew."

A gamble he would have won. As Dumarest led the way to where a plank bridge crossed the ditch men stepped from a hut at its end.

"Hold it!" The officer, like his men, wore a uniform and was armed. "It's late—you got business in town?"

"Nothing special." Dumarest glanced toward the field. "Just wanted to check on the chance of getting a berth."

"Leave it until tomorrow." The officer rested a hand on the pistol holstered at his waist. "Curfew runs from an hour before sunset to an hour after dawn. You should know that."

"We've been helping the monks," said Angado. "Do you police inside?"

"Hell, no." The officer echoed his contempt. "You scum take care of yourselves."

In more ways than one.

Dumarest heard the shout of pain as he neared a hovel sprouting like an ugly growth at the edge of the cluster. A man answered it as it came again.

"Steady! Hold still, you fool! Damn it, Susan, get help!"

A woman burst from the door and stared at them with wild eyes. She was gaunt, dressed in rags, an ugly blotch marring one cheek. Flecks of blood stained her hands and naked forearms.

"Please!" She looked from Dumarest to Angado. "My man! He's hurt bad! Jacek is trying but needs help! Please!"

Inside the gloom was thick, relieved only by the guttering light of a wick floating in a cup of oil. On a heap of rags a man lay writhing, another kneeling at his side. Like the woman, his hands and wrists were stained with blood.

"Hold him!" he snapped after one glance at the visitors. "Grab him tight."

Dumarest said, without moving, "What's wrong with him?"

"He tripped and fell into a bed of feathers." Jacek's tone was sarcastic. "That's how he got that face."

The nose was broken, the lips split, the chin caked with blood. The eyes were puffed and the forehead bruised. Whoever had beaten the man had done a vicious job.

"Gengiz?"

"His boys. Breck fell behind on his payments. They warned him once but he still couldn't find the cash. So they worked him over. Smashed his face, cracked some ribs and twisted his arm out of its socket. I'm trying to get it back."

The hard way, working with strength but little skill. Dumarest gestured him aside, took his place, examined the injured limb. The dislocation was severe, the joint badly swollen. The injured man groaned as Dumarest moved his hands.

"How long?"

"Since noon. I had to wait for Jacek to get back."

Angado said, "Couldn't you have sent for trained help?"

"Medics won't come into Lowtown. They'll treat you if you can get to them but first they want paying." Breck was patient despite his pain, talking as if to a child. "I can't pay. If I had money I wouldn't be in this mess."

The woman said, "Can you help him? If you can for God's sake get to work."

"Hold his legs, Jacek. Angado, you hold his other arm.

Keep him turned on his side." Dumarest picked up a mess of rag and wadded it into a ball. "This is going to hurt," he warned. "But it'll soon be over. Just try to relax. Take some deep breaths. Got anything to bite on?"

"Here." The woman thrust a stick between Breck's jaws. "Don't hurt him too much, mister."

Dumarest placed the wadded ball between the upper arm of the injured man and the torso, setting it high beneath the armpit to act as a fulcrum. Checking its position he adjusted the limb then, without warning, thrust down hard on the elbow.

Breck strained, biting into the wood, a low, animal-like groan coming from his throat. Sound Dumarest ignored as he fought the pull of muscles, maintaining the leverage as he felt the swollen joint. A moment as he rammed the heel of his hand against the spot, then he felt the joint slip back into place.

"Good." He rested a hand on Breck's sweating forehead. "It's all over," he said. "Just relax now."

"It hurts."

"The pain will go but it'll be sore for a while." Dumarest ripped rags into strips and bound the arm and shoulder in a constricting web, tying the arm hard against the chest. "That'll help the ribs, too." He looked at Jacek. "The next time anyone gets into trouble take them to the monks."

"I did my best."

"I know, but you lack training. They've had it." Dumarest added, "I guess you know how to take care of his nose."

"I should." Jacek's own was twisted across his face. "I've had to fix mine often enough. The rest of the cuts too. It was just that shoulder which beat me. A neat trick that; you using the arm itself as a lever." He paused then said. "Not that it'll do much good."

"Gengiz?" Dumarest shrugged. "A few of you could get together and take care of his boys."

"There'll be others." Jacek's tone reflected his loss of spirit. "There are always others."

Angado said, "What happens if he still can't pay? Will they kill him?"

"Not unless they have to. There are mines to the north and

a ready market for workers. Deliver a volunteer and collect a bonus. Gengiz has a habit of delivering volunteers."

Dumarest looked at the interior of the hovel. "Maybe a man could do worse."

"I'm not signing a contract!" Breck struggled to sit upright on the rags. "Once they get you they never let go."

"You'd eat," said Dumarest. "You and your woman. What better have you got here?"

"I'm free!"

"Sure," said Dumarest. "I'd forgotten. Maybe Gengiz has too."

He moved to the opening and stepped out into the thickening purple haze of the dying day. After a moment Angado joined him, falling into step alongside as Dumarest moved along the littered path. In the shadows rodents scuttled and, from a shack, came a snatch of discordant song.

As it died Dumarest said, "You gave Breck money, right? It was a mistake."

"It was my money."

"It was still a mistake. Now he's not as desperate as he was. He'll pay and buy his way out of trouble. But it'll return and he'll be back where he started."

"I've given him time, at least. His shoulder will heal and maybe he can find a job." Angado looked at his companion. "Would you pay, Earl? If Gengiz makes his demand will you meet it?"

"I might."

"Then how can you blame Breck and those like him for doing the same?"

"I'm not blaming them," said Dumarest. "They can do as they like. It's none of my business. But if I was starving and had a woman depending on me and she was starving too and some thug came and tried to rob me—well, who knows?"

They reached the end of the path, turned left, moved into a cleared space formed by the junction of crossings, headed up a slope to where the church rose against the sky.

Before it, silhouetted against the brightly colored plastic, two men were beating a robed figure to the ground.

It was a scene from nightmare, the men tall, broad, their clubs the yard-long weapons carried by Gengiz's guard. The monk was crouched, hands lifted to protect his face, body bowed as if he were a suppliant accepting a merited penance.

A stagelike vista broken as Angado yelled and ran forward.

"Stop that! Stop it! Leave him alone!"

A command obeyed only momentarily as the men turned at the shout, clubs lifted, contemptuous of the new arrivals.

Dumarest said, sharply, "Angado! Leave it!"

An order ignored if heard and he ran in turn, passing the other, heading to where he had left the broom leaning against the fabric of the church. Set far to one side of where the men stood over the monk he was ignored. As he snatched it up Angado came to a halt.

"Back off!" His breath was ragged, his voice hard but shaking a little. "You filth! Beating up a monk! Is that the best you can do?"

He was talking instead of acting, a mistake repeated by the thugs.

"Listen to the insect." The man on the right hefted his club. "Doesn't all that big talk frighten you, Rayne? Maybe we should get down on our knees and beg his forgiveness."

"Maybe we should, Kay." The other thug played along. "For all we know this thing could be his father." His foot kicked at the monk. "I've heard they have some strange ideas of how things should be done."

"We could make them show us, eh? If—"

Rayne broke off as Dumarest came running toward him, broom in hand, the wide fan of bristles aimed at his eyes. Spines which circled to avoid the sweep of his club and dug into cheeks and forehead. Lifting as Dumarest reversed the pole to send it rising sharply between the thighs to smash against the groin. As the thug doubled, retching, the end of the pole slammed into his throat, rupturing the larynx and filling the windpipe with blood and congested tissue.

As he fell Angado lunged at the other man.

He had his knife in his hand, the point slanted upward, thumb to the blade as he had seen trained fighters do in a dozen arenas. A hold, stance and motion designed to deliver a killing thrust. But he was slow. Slow!

Dumarest saw the lifted club, the practiced response of a man who had made violence his trade. Held like a sword the weapon gave him the advantage. Before he could drive the knife home Angado would be dead.

Dumarest yelled, throwing the broom as he yelled, the sound shocking in its harsh timbre. As the thug slowed his advance the pole, hurtling like a spear, glided between his legs causing him to stumble, to fall helplessly on the lifted blade of Angado's knife.

As the thug twitched, spilling his life in a carmine flood, Dumarest said, bitterly, "Well, I hope you're satisfied."

"It was him or me, Earl."

"It needn't have been either. You shouldn't have interfered."

"They were beating up a helpless man. A monk!"

"That makes them special?" Dumarest shrugged as Angado made no answer. "Well, it happened, let's get him inside."

Pollard had taken the beating but he wasn't the only one in the infirmary. Dexter lay on another cot, supine, his eyes closed, hands lying limp at his side. A bandage made a white swath across his forehead.

"Concussion," explained Kollar. "A cracked clavicle and a badly bruised elbow. In that he was lucky."

"When?"

"About thirty minutes ago. Two men arrived and demanded to see him. Brother Dexter guessed what they wanted and ordered us not to interfere. After the attack they left and we brought him inside. Then they returned and Brother Pollard went out to remonstrate with them. The rest you know."

Dumarest said, "You stood by while they beat up an old man?"

"We had no choice."

"You could have gone out there. Shouted. Gathered a crowd if nothing else."

"No," said Angado. "They couldn't. They were under orders and had to obey." He looked at the limp figure lying on the cot, at the groaning shape of the younger monk. "Gengiz cheated. He gave them until sunset. The attack took place before then. Brother Dexter must have thought they came to talk. In any case he would have wanted to avoid a battle."

Taking the beating himself. Willingly offering his own body as a sacrifice. A waste—the men who'd attacked him had lost the meaning of shame as had the man who'd sent them.

"It's the way of the Church," said Angado, "to follow a policy of nonviolence no matter what the cost. If the church here is to succeed then others must protect it. Those who value it and find comfort in its teachings. Once a congregation has been established there'll be no need for the monks to prove themselves. They'll have been accepted. After that the rest will follow."

"Until it does?" Dumarest didn't wait for an answer. "Never mind. I wanted us to stay out of this but now we have no choice. You took care of that. Those thugs are dead and others would have seen how they died. Now we're both marked men." He looked at the monk. "Find us two robes. Large ones."

Kollar shook his head. "I'm sorry, but Brother Dexter made it clear—"

"Look at him now," snapped Dumarest. "Do you want others to join him? But if your conscience troubles you let's do it this way." He spoke directly at the unconscious monk. "Brother Dexter, do you object to us using a couple of robes?" He waited, listening, then looked again at Kollar. "You see, he didn't object."

"But—"

"Get them!" Dumarest looked at the injured men then at Angado. "Violence," he said bleakly. "It's everywhere. The strong bearing down on the weak with demands and threats. Scum like Gengiz or some puffed up lordling or a faceless bureaucrat all issuing their orders. Pay or be punished. Obey or suffer fines, imprisonment, execution. Well, to hell with them. There's only one way they can be stopped." He looked at the robes Kollar had fetched. "Good. Now, Brother, go outside and bring in those clubs."

As Dumarest had expected the clubs were weighted with lead. Long, slender wands with the vicious capacity to shatter a skull or snap a bone. He hefted one, sent it whining through the air, lifted it in a curve, sent it darting forward to halt an inch from Angado's chest.

"Fast," he said. "See?"

"What are you trying to tell me?"

"When you decide to act don't hesitate. That's the mistake you made out there. Don't waste time in talk. Attack, do it fast and don't be gentle. A hurt man can hit back, a dead one can't. Now hit me with your club." Dumarest shook his head as Angado lifted the weapon, his own reaching out to jab hard against the other's chest. "Not like that. It leaves you too open. Thrust as I did."

Angado was slow. Dumarest swept aside the club and jabbed again. The next attack was faster, the club circling to avoid the parry. Dumarest knocked it far to the opposite side, jabbed, stood waiting.

"Earl, I—"

"Don't talk! Act! Kill me before I kill you! Move, damn you! Move!"

Hard practice within the body of the church, sweating inside the hampering robes, learning how to compensate for the heavy material. As they moved the axe fell from Angado's belt, Dumarest picking it up and thrusting it beneath his robe. Finally he called a halt.

"That's enough. We'll rest for a while."

"Do you think I've improved?"

"You're better." Angado was still slow but had lost his initial hesitation. Dumarest said, "You killed a man tonight. Was he your first?"

"There was another. We had an argument and he came for me. It was an accident, really, he had a gun and I grabbed at it and it went off and shot him in the chest. A laser. The stink of burned flesh stuck in my nose for days." Angado paused then said, "I suppose you find killing easy."

"No," said Dumarest. "It's never that."

"But you intend to kill again."

"You've left me no choice—I told you why. Gengiz has to dispose of us as a matter of pride. He's got a good thing going here and others know it. Once he shows weakness they'll try to take over. So we have to go. As we can't avoid it we have to meet it. Pick our own time and place."

"But why the robes?"

Dumarest shrugged, "It gives us an edge—who's afraid of a monk?"

They rested, dozing, waiting for the dawn. The best time to attack when the guards would be sleepy and Gengiz unaware.

In the infirmary Brother Kollar kept vigil over the sick, two of the other monks sleeping, the third standing awake in case of need. Dumarest started fully alert as a hand touched his shoulder. In the dim light he saw the strained face of Brother Galpin.

"Something is wrong," whispered the monk. "There are people outside."

"Suppliants?"

"No. I think they intend to rob us."

Thieves working under Gengiz or others eager to seize an opportunity. The dead thugs, untouched where they lay, no longer served to keep the vultures at bay.

Dumarest rose, stretched, looked at the translucent roof of the church. The stars, paling, had left a blurred glow and he sensed it must be close to dawn. Others knew the best time to attack.

They could be heard working at the wall to one side. A rasp of metal against the stubborn plastic the sound like the ugly grating of teeth. Dumarest crossed to it, knelt, listened, looked to the other side.

Angado said, "Wouldn't they break directly into the storeroom?"

"If they knew just where it was," agreed Dumarest. "Or if that's all they wanted."

"You think they're after us?"

"Gengiz knows we're in here. We killed his men. Now he has the chance to kill us and wreck the church at the same time. If monks die we'll be blamed. Either way he can't lose."

"The church eliminated and used us as an example of what happens if anyone steps out of line." Angado drew in his breath. "We shouldn't be here, Earl. Nor wearing these robes. The monks don't deserve this."

"If you're tired of life just strip and walk outside." Dumarest was curt. "If you're not just shut up and listen."

The grating had grown louder, a sound impossible to miss and one sure to attract attention. Dumarest moved to the far wall where, dimly, he could see the vague outline of shadows.

"Here," he whispered to Angado. "They're coming through here. Remember what I told you."

"Are you going to attack without warning?"

"I thought you'd learned."

"Sorry. I wasn't thinking."

"Don't think," advised Dumarest. "Just act. Hit hard and fast." He shifted the grip on his club. "Here they come!"

The wall opened like a flower, petals of plastic parting to reveal a cluster of shapes, men who ran forward, metal glinting in their hands.

The first went down, choking, vomiting from savage thrusts to throat and stomach. Others follwed them as the clubs whined through the air to land on shoulders, backs, skulls. Victims of a ferocious and totally unexpected defense. Monks did not fight, yet monks seemed to be everywhere; in the dark interior of the church only the robed figures could be seen.

Calm followed the violence, a period that Dumarest knew would be followed by a more calculated attack. One which, surprise now lost, would give numbers the advantage.

He blinked as a vivid beam of light streamed from outside to illuminate the scene.

It came from where Gengiz stood at a distance from the structure, a powerful flashlight in one hand, a laser in the other. The pale light of dawn gave him a somber appearance, accentuated by his scowl and the weapon in his hand.

He fired as Dumarest watched, the beam searing plastic, burning a hole high and to one side.

"Drop those clubs!" The laser fired again adding a second hole to the first. "Drop them, I say!"

Again the laser vented its energy, closer this time, and Angado grunted as he slapped at the smoke rising from the edge of his robe.

"Your last warning! Drop those clubs!"

"Earl?"

"Do it!"

His own club followed Angado's to the floor, his eyes narrowed as he assessed the situation. The attackers had dropped at the signal of the firing, hugging the ground to give Gengiz an open field. The man himself stood too far away to be reached by a thrown knife even if the blade could travel fast enough to beat the speed of his finger. The clubs were gone.

"Raise your hands," said Dumarest quietly. "Walk toward Gengiz. Stumble a little as if you're hurt. Beg if you want but do what he tells you."

Angado threw him a glance then obeyed. He was a good actor. Dumarest followed him, stooped, one leg dragging, a hand clutching his chest.

"Please!" Angado turned his raised hands palms outward, the fingers spread to demonstrate his defenselessness. "Don't hurt me. I had nothing to do with this. Look, I've got money, I'll pay—"

"Shut up!" The muzzle of the laser remained aimed at his stomach. "Move over to one side. Faster." The gun signaled the direction, the beam of the flashlight searing into Angado's face. "You're not a monk. I know you. You killed my boys. You and—" The beam of the flashlight moved to Dumarest. He was crouched even lower, one hand pressed to his stomach, lurching as he moved forward. "Hold it!" Gengiz snarled as he recognized the face in the vivid light. "You're the other one. But why the robes? What the hell's going on?"

"Money," said Dumarest. "The monks had it. We wanted it. Now we've got it. If you hadn't arrived we'd have got away. The guards wouldn't argue with a couple of monks breaking curfew. Not now it's after dawn."

"Money?"

"Sure. A lot of it. Show him, Angado."

Dumarest moved as Gengiz turned toward the other man, flashlight and laser shifting targets. Both jerking back as, too late, he realized the mistake he'd made.

The distance was too great for a knife even if he could have snatched it from his boot, but the axe had extra weight. Dumarest tore it from his belt, lifted it, threw it with all his strength as Gengiz turned. Smoke and flame spurted from his robe as the laser fired then Gengiz was down, the axe buried in his skull, blood and brains making a red-gray patina on his face.

"Hold it!" Dumarest yelled at the men coming from the church. "He's dead! You want to join him?"

He faced them, the laser he'd scooped up steady in his hand, searing the ground inches from the boots of the nearest man. Firing repeatedly until the men ran in panic, leaving them alone with the damaged church, the staring monks, the uncaring dead.

Chapter Eight

This time it was different; instead of the bizarre landscape with the solitary figure of the Cyber Prime there was a vaulted hall, a dais holding three thronelike chairs occupied by figures adorned with legalistic robes. A tribunal seated as if in judgment, faces dimmed and blurred in the flickering light of flambeaux. But if the scene was different the shock was the same.

Avro drew in his breath and looked at his hands. Air filled his lungs and the hands were his own as were the feet, the arms, the robe which clothed his body. One now lying as if dead in his cabin on the ship resting on the surface of Velor.

What was happening to him?

Rapport was never like this and, since the time when he had apparently spoken to Marle, it had been as always. The contact, the exchange, the euphoria which yielded ecstasy and which resulted from electromagnetic stimulation of the pleasure center of the brain.

A thought which startled him—was it true? And why should it have come to him at all?

"Cyber Avro you may speak." The central figure lifted a hand, let it fall back to the arm of the chair, to grip it with long, spatulate fingers. "Your report?"

One which could have been transmitted with the speed of thought now having to be vocalized.

Avro was brief, ending with the finding of the grave. "The body was in the final stages of dissolution. Little remained but a skeleton and identification was impossible."

"The size?"

"Fitted the characteristics of both men dumped from the

Thorn." Unnecessary detail—he had said that identification was impossible. Inefficiency compounded as he added, "The bones had been badly fretted but fitted the structure-scale relevant to the search. More could have been learned had we discovered the grave sooner."

"Obviously." The tone was dry. "Continue."

"The grave was on the site of what had been a camp. Radiated heat from the colony of scavenger beetles which had congregated on the spot registered on our instruments. The immediate terrain showed signs of having been stripped of fuel, and ash was found beneath a layer of sand. To one side, also beneath windblown sand, was found what could have been the landing spot of a vessel. Tests in the lower soil-strata confirm the size and weight of an object which could have been a ship." Avro paused, seeing again the glinting mass of chitin from the insects attracted to the water and food held in the body. The bones which first had seemed to be fashioned from tiny, mobile gems, turning gray and dusty as the scavengers fled from the light. The landing spot had been a ragged scar. "Tests revealed radiation levels in the local soil consistent with the generation of an Erhaft field."

"Your conclusions?"

"A vessel landed. A man was buried. The vessel departed."

It was not enough and Avro knew it but there was reason for his brevity. Before him the seated figure stirred, those to either side remaining as motionless as before. Were they nothing but a part of the illusion? An addition to the flambeaux, the dais, the thrones, the vaulted chamber?

It had to be illusion—but the central figure?

It stirred again and Avro caught the impression of a host of faces blurring one into the other to form a montage at once familiar and strange. People he had known, cybers long gone to their reward, now the brains forming Central Intelligence. Was this the product of some dreaming mind toying with the creation of new frames of reference? The fruit of a whim?

Of madness?

"Brevity is always to be desired," said his inquisitor. "But brevity, carried to the extreme, verges on stupidity. Which vessel? What man? Elucidate."

"The vessel is unknown," said Avro. "Working on the assumption that it could have been in distress, a wide search was made in order to determine if any radio signal had been received. The results were negative. The settlements on Velor lay to the far side of the plateau—I have described the terrain.''

"And?"

"The man is also unknown. The probability that it is Dumarest is in the order of fifty percent. Two men were dumped," he explained. "Either could have died.''

"Or,'' said the central figure, "it could have been someone from the vessel.''

The obvious and Avro felt again the sickening sense of failure he had once known as a boy when new to the Cyclan. Even as he watched the dais blurred, the chamber, both becoming the bleak room in which he had sat for initial testing and tuition.

"You.'' The man who had sat on a throne now stood behind a desk, warmly scarlet in his robe, his face one Avro would never forget. Cyber Cadell, coldly unforgiving, relentless in weeding out the unsuitable. "Come here and tell me if these are the same.''

Three blocks of plastic rested on the desk before him, all apparently identical. Avro stared at them, checking shape, color and size.

"Well?"

"Master, they are the same.''

Cadell said nothing but his hand turned over the blocks. The lower side of each was colored differently from the rest and no color was the same.

"Master! I—''

"You jumped to a false conclusion based on insufficient data. I did not say you were not allowed to touch them for a complete examination. A fault. Repeat it and the Cyclan will have no further use for you.''

The room dissolved, became again the vaulted chamber, but Cadell remained, his face replacing the blurred visage of the inquisitor.

He said, "The ramifications of the problem are such that any prediction would be of such a low order of probability as to be almost valueless. The dead man could have come from the vessel; a passenger or a member of the crew. He could have been Dumarest or his companion. The grave itself need have nothing to do with either the ship or the man you are hunting. Coincidences do happen.''

Another test? Avro remembered the bleak room, the blocks of plastic, the same cold, watchful eyes of the tutor. It was tempting to accept the suggestion; coincidences *did* happen, but he knew this was not one of them. A conviction on the intuitive level as strong as that which told him Dumarest was still alive.

But where? Where?

Ryder had cheated; the fee he'd paid over and above passage for work on the generator had been made up of cash and a pair of heavy bracelets ornately designed and studded with gems. The design was genuine but the metal was dross thinly plated with gold, the gems glass.

"Fifty zobars." The jeweler had the visage of an old and weary bird of prey. "Fifty—and I'm being generous."

Angado said, "You're robbing us."

"Did I ask you to come to me? Am I making you stay?" The jeweler's shoulders lifted as if they had been wings. "Try elsewhere if you want but you'll get no better offer. Ladies here demand items of genuine worth and the poor cannot afford costly baubles. To sell them I must wait for a harlot with a bemused client or a lovesick fool eager to impress his mistress. Fifty zobars. That's my final offer."

One raised to sixty as they reached the door, doubled when Dumarest added the laser Gengiz had used.

Outside he headed for the baths. The robes had been discarded but the taint of violent exertion remained as did the stench of Lowtown. Both vanished in clouds of scented steam, icy showers, hot-rooms inducing a copious sweat. A nubile girl led them to a private cubicle.

"Here you can rest, my lords. If you should require a massage I shall be happy to attend you."

Angado said, quickly, "No. Just leave the oil. We'll manage the rest."

"As you wish, my lord." Her tone was flat, devoid of emotion, but her eyes held a worldly understanding. "Some wine, perhaps? Stimulants? If there is anything you should require just press the bell."

The button which gave access to a host of pleasures and all at a price.

Dumarest relaxed on the couch, sweat dewing his naked body, hanging like pearls on the cicatrices marking his torso. Old scars long healed to thin, livid welts. Angado touched them, his fingers smooth with oil, pressing as they followed the line of muscle. His own body, unmarked, wore a halo of mist generated by the heat and illuminated by overhead lights.

"Hold still, Earl, you've a knot there!" His fingers probed, eased, moved on with skilled assurance. "I learned massage in the gynmasium at the university. Most students were short of funds and we saved by each treating the other. The instructors insisted we intersperse bouts of study with althetic pursuits so there were plenty of strained joints, pulled muscles and the like to take care of." His hands roved over the shoulders, the chest, the stomach. "These scars, Earl. The arena?"

Dumarest rolled over to lie on his face.

"The arena," said Angado. "None on your back so you had to be facing your opponent. And the way you fought showed skill. The way you taught me, too." His oiled thumbs ran up the sides, dug into the declivities alongside the spine. "But I'll never be as good as you are. Nor as fast." His hands fell to his sides. "That should do it. You want to rub me?"

"Call the girl."

"No." Angado mounted his own couch. "I'll do without." He lay silent for a while then said, "I've only seen two other men scarred like you. One was a fighter and I saw him in the arena on Rorsan. Kreagan, I think he was called, a big man, moved like a cat. A left-hander as I remember. He fought and won and afterward I bought him wine. He got a little drunk and started to boast. Said he could take on any three ordinary men at the same time. He also claimed there was nothing to match the excitement of facing an opponent. He said it was better than going with a woman." He turned on his couch to face Dumarest. "Was he right, Earl? Is it like that?"

"For some, maybe."

"And you?"

Dumarest said, "What happened to your friend?"

"Kreagan? He died shortly afterward. But—" Angado

broke off. "I see. Fighting isn't a game and it isn't like going with a woman. Make one mistake and it's your last. Right?"

"Yes." Dumarest looked at the floor beneath the couch, one set with a variety of colored squares. Turning he looked at the ceiling with its mass of abstract designs. Patterns designed to soothe and induce a restful somnolence. One negated by Angado. He said, "Who was the other man?"

The one with the scars? A monk. Brother Lyndom. He was old and was giving me tuition. We went swimming one day and I saw his body. It was horrible. All seared and puckered as if burned and torn. Later I learned that he'd been tortured on some world where he'd gone to set up a church but when I asked him what had happened he just laughed and said he'd run into a swarm of angry bees. I guess that's why I respect monks. I wanted to be one once, but that was before I learned I had no real choice in determining my future. And perhaps it wasn't in me. I'm too much of a coward to face what they put up with."

"Most are." Dumarest reared to sit upright then threw his legs over the edge of the couch. "Where's that oil?"

It was warm, scented, slippery beneath his hands as they moved against the other's body. His fingers, stronger, if lacking the fine skill an expert would possess, dug deep into fat and muscle.

As Angado relaxed he said, "Was the monk with your people on Lychen?"

"That's right."

"What happened?" Dumarest filled his palms with more oil. "What made you leave home?"

"It's an old story. My father married late and was old when I was born. He died in a crash and my mother with him. My uncle took over until I became of age. By then Perotto had become the real head. I tried to take over but couldn't manage." Angado stirred beneath Dumarest's hands. "Maybe I should have fought harder but I didn't know how. So I compromised."

"And?"

"I drifted. Just traveled around. What else?"

"There's no harm in that." Dumarest slapped a thigh and began to knead Angado's back as he turned over to lie prone

on the couch. "The trouble is it doesn't get you anywhere.
Ever think of going back?"

"To Lychen? No. That was the deal."

"Deals can be changed. Don't you ever get homesick?"

"No. Do you?"

"Often." Dumarest moved his hands up to the base of the
neck and probed at the tension he found there. "So where
will you go? There's not much here on Yuanka."

"I guess not." Angado lay silent for a while, speaking as
Dumarest lowered his hands to the shoulders. "You saved
my life," he said abruptly. "I'm not forgetting that."

"So?"

"You don't have to be stranded here. We could travel
together. I've always wished I had a companion and we seem
to get along. Just as if you were my older brother." He
forced lightness into his tone. "I've always wanted an older
brother. As a kid I was always alone and after my parents
went—well, uncle did his best but it wasn't the same. Anyway,
I owe you."

The truth and Dumarest didn't argue. "It takes money to
buy passage."

"You don't have to tell me that." Angado twisted his head
to look upward, smiling, confident he would get his own
way. "We've been robbed and cheated but it doesn't matter.
I've got money. As much as we need. All I have to do is get
it. Earl?" His smile widened as Dumarest nodded. "Then it's
a deal. Good. Let's be on our way."

Credit Debutin had branches scattered throughout the
Burdinnion and that on Yuanka occupied a prominent position on the main plaza. Dumarest waited outside as Angado
entered, looking at the shops ringing the area, the familiar
figure standing outside the casino. Brother Lloyd, somber in
his robe, a bowl of chipped plastic in his hand, was busy
collecting alms.

A good position, as he knew; gamblers were superstitious
when it came to luck. A coin on entering could placate the
goddess of fortune and if you were successful another was
her just tribute. Even losers dropped a coin in the bowl in the
hope of bettering future chances.

"Earl!" Angado came from the bank, his face drawn. "I don't understand it," he said. "I just don't understand it."

"No money?"

"No, but—"

"Leave it." A cafe stood to one side and Dumarest led the way toward it. At a table he ordered a pot of tisane and waited until it had been served and poured before looking at his companion. "No money," he said. "Did they tell you why?"

"Yes, but it's crazy. The account's been stopped. I can't understand it. The arrangement was plain; I can draw at any branch of Credit Debutin against the family account. Five thousand ryall a month. That's Lychen currency," he explained. "It's converted to local."

"How many zobars would that be?"

"Over ten thousand." Angado met Dumarest's eyes. "I told you I had money."

Dumarest said, "Have you an account? A credit balance?" His right hand moved toward his left forearm checking as he halted the subconscious gesture. "Any money at all?"

"Only what we split." Angado looked helplessly at the tisane. "I can't understand it. Perotto gave me his word and there's never been any difficulty before. Just my name, thumb-print and code number and the cash is handed over." His hand clenched, slammed down on the table with force enough to send tisane slopping from the cups. "What the hell's going on?"

The waitress came from within the cafe, attracted by the noise, frowning at the mess. Dumarest dropped coins on the table. "For your trouble," he explained. "Would you bring me a sheet of notepaper? Nothing special, a leaf from a book will do."

The paper was thick, rough, jagged down one edge. Dumarest placed it on the table before Angado.

"Write me a promissory note. It's a gambling debt for five hundred and date it before we were dumped. No," he amended. "Earlier than that. Before you took passage on the *Thorn*."

"When I was on Tysa?"

"That'll do." Dumarest took the paper when Angado had finished. He folded it, opened it, dropped it on the ground and trod on it. Picking it up he scuffed the sheet and stained it with tisane. Folding it again he tucked it under his tunic and rested it beneath his armpit. "How did they treat you in there?"

"The bank?" Angado scowled. "Like dirt!"

"I want the truth."

"They were cold. Hostile, even. They just said there was no account and no funds for me. I argued but got nowhere. The instructions had been revoked and no money would be paid."

"Did they check you out? Your thumbprint or—"

"No. Nothing. They just weren't interested. I can't understand it. Perotto swore that—what the hell's gone wrong?"

"Think about it," advised Dumarest. "Now let's see if I can cash this note."

The man behind the counter was snobbishly supercilious. He picked up the paper with caution, nose wrinkling at the odor of human perspiration, unfolding it as if it could bite.

"Yours?"

"It's mine." Dumarest leaned over the counter thrusting his face toward the other. "A bearer promissory note, right? You pay whoever presents it. I'm presenting it."

"I meant was it issued to you?"

"It's a bearer note." Dumarest let impatience edge his tone. "What the hell does it matter who it was issued to? I've got it. Check it out and give me the money."

"If you'd like to wait? Come back later—"

"Now!" Dumarest looked beyond the man. "You the boss here? If you can't handle the job maybe I'd better speak to someone who can."

He relaxed as the man hurried away to confer with others. The note was genuine, drawn on the Credit Debutin, carrying Angado's signature, code number and thumbprint. Those details could be checked against the computer data in the bank. He straightened as the cashier returned, another man at his side. One who waited until they were alone.

"Mister—?" He shrugged as Dumarest made no answer. "No matter. I'm the manager here and I'm afraid I have bad news for you. This note of yours cannot be met."

"You mean it's a fake?"

"No, I'm not saying that. It seems genuine enough and

normally I'd accept it but there are no longer funds to meet it.''

''He's broke?''

''Not broke—dead. The account has been closed.'' Frowning the manager added, ''It's odd. You're the second man who's come in asking about that account. The other claimed to be the person himself.''

''Maybe he was.''

''Impossible. The report from head office was most explicit. That's why no money can be paid against that note. Of course you can make due representation to the estate for settlement but that will take time. My advice to you is to sell it. You'll have to take a loss, naturally, but—''

''Sell it? Who the hell would buy junk like this?''

''At a quarter. face value?'' The manager met Dumarest's eyes. ''I would for one—the Karroum own most of Lychen.''

Chapter Nine

Angado had gone when Dumarest emerged from the bank, the monk seated in his place. Brother Lloyd looked tired, grateful for the tisane he had been given. As Dumarest approached he looked up and began to rise from his chair.

"Sit down." Dumarest dropped into the space facing him. "Did he leave word?"

"Yes. He's in there." The monk gestured toward the casino. "He said to be sure and tell you where he had gone."

A fool unable to restrain his impatience and seeking novelty to pass the time. Dumarest helped himself to some of the tisane and leaned back in his chair as he sipped the fragrant brew. Thoughtful as he reviewed the situation.

Angado was a liability and yet it was hard to think of him as such. A danger; those who wanted him dead would try again and to be close was to invite disaster. A man now without assets and only one proven skill. Yet he held potential value; the resources of his House and Family. Wealth, influence, power—things Dumarest could use in his search for Earth and that search could begin on Lychen where Angado belonged.

He stood at a table, face flushed with excitement as he watched the bounding progress of a ball. One which bounced at the edges of ranked divisions to hover and finally come to rest.

"Red. Even. Eighteen." The croupier's voice was a drone. "Place your bets."

Angado had lost. He lost again. As he went to put more coins on the board Dumarest caught his arm.

"We need to talk."

"You're back! Good!" Angado smiled his pleasure. "One more turn and I'll be with you."

"Now!"

"One more turn."

He played and lost and ordered wine as he led the way to a table set in an alcove flanked with mirrors. The girl who brought it was young, enticing in her slit gown, smiling as she saw her tip.

"Anything else, my lord?"

"Food. A plate of delicacies. The best."

"No food." Dumarest was harsh. "Not yet." Then, as Angado made to protest, he added, savagely, "Do as you like after we've spoken. Now we have things to settle. Why didn't you tell me you were rich?"

"I'm not. I told you about the arrangement. Anyway, what does it matter?" Angado sipped, drank, refilled his glass. "Drink up, Earl, enjoy yourself. We can afford it."

"No."

"Why not? You got the money, didn't you?"

"A quarter of face value." Dumarest stacked coins on the table. "Your share. All you're going to get. If you want to squander it go ahead. It's your money."

Looking at it Angado said, slowly, "What are you telling me?"

"You're dead. Officially dead. No cash and no credit. Your notes won't be met. From now on you make your own way." Dumarest picked up his glass, lifted it in a mock toast. "Freedom, Angado. Let's drink to it—you can't afford to waste the wine."

He watched as Angado obeyed, the truth swallowed with the ruby liquid, cold realization dampening the euphoria of alcohol. As yet life to Angado had been an adventure, one padded by the cushions of wealth, now those cushions had been tweaked away and he was going to get hurt.

Dumarest said, "Think of Lowtown. Remember it. That's where you could wind up unless you're careful. Bear it in mind, the dirt, the stink, the decay." The grinding poverty, the pain, the desperation. An alien world to one accustomed to riches. A hostile one to a man arrogant with the memory of wealth. "Do you still feel hungry?"

Angado shook his head, remembering the cost of the wine, the loss at the table.

"What are you going to do?"

"Get back to Lychen. There has to be some mistake. Perotto will correct it. He—"

"Wants you dead!" snapped Dumarest. "And you're a fool not to see it. Remain a fool and you'll die alone. I mean it."

"You'll leave me?"

"I've no time for a man who refuses to help himself. You're dead, Angado. It's only a matter of time before you're in the ground. That's just what will happen when you meet Perotto unless—" He broke off and waited for the other to recognize the obvious.

"I've got to get back home," said Angado. "But without Perotto suspecting I'm back until I'm ready to face him. You'll come with me, Earl? Help me?" Anxiety tinged his voice as Dumarest remained silent. "You won't regret it. I swear to that. I'll give you anything you want."

The gratitude of princes—but first it had to be earned.

Larbi Vargas was old, wizened, his face seamed with a mesh of lines as if it had been leather unoiled and left too long in the sun. Only his eyes were young, holding a shrewd brilliance, one which matched the razor-edged keenness of his mind. An entrepreneur, an agent, a go-between. A man like a spider sitting in a web of information. One drifting in the dim region lying in the strata between law and lawlessness, order and chaos. Men like him existed on every world and Dumarest had known how to track him down. To Angado he was an alien form of life.

Now he watched as the preliminaries were completed; the small cakes eaten with wine. The pleasantries. The handing over of scarce resources.

"You are a man after my own heart," said Vargas. He wiped a crumb from his lips. "Too many who come to me are impatient. They neglect the niceties of civilized conduct but you, obviously, are aware of ancient traditions. Some more wine?"

"Thank you, no."

"You?" Vargas sighed and lowered the bottle as Angado

shook his head. "Your problem is a common one, my friends. How to escape a hostile world? Money is the answer, the key to all things. How to get it? That is a harder problem. Theft is difficult and dangerous but desperate men are willing to accept risks. If you are such something could be arranged. No?"

"No."

"Then let us examine other prospects. Work at the mines is available but only for those willing to sign a contract. They pay is low and expenses high. I would not advise it. A party left last week for the northern hills to hunt kulighin. A beast as large as a man," he explained. "Vicious, cunning, valued for its hide and certain glands. Always some die on such a hunt and reward is never certain. But your stake is large enough to buy you a place in such a party if you can match it with experience and would be willing to take a lower share."

"Too long," said Dumarest. "We want something fast. Passage on a ship heading to Lychen. One needing an engineer would be ideal."

"Every vessel operating in the Burdinnion needs engineers," said Vargas dryly. "Which is why all ships carry them. If you were a captain would you trust your life and ship to an unknown? Someone lacking the years in which to have gained experience and without documents to prove his ability? Of course," he added, "such documents could be provided."

In time and with money they couldn't spare. Things the old man knew but he worked in his own way and to press him would lessen his desire to cooperate.

Now he said, "For one of you there is no real problem. If you just want passage away from Yuanka and are willing to do what is asked and spend what you have on bribes there are several ships on which I could arrange a passage. The *Warton* bound for Lorne. The *Koura* bound for Balaban. A handler who can run a table and show a profit would be accepted." His eyes rested on Dumarest. "And there would be no need for him to pass through the gate."

An extra bonus and an essential one for any wanted criminal.

Angado said, quickly, "We must travel together."

"Then your choice is limited. The *Audran* leaves tomorrow at dawn. They carry a cargo of mikha and need men to tend them. For the right price the captain will allow you to work your passage."

"To where?"

"Haroun." Vargas shrugged as Angado shook his head. "The choice is yours but I suggest you take it. Haroun is less hostile than Yuanka."

"The mikha?"

"A low order of life similar to leeches." Vargas added, with the hint of a smile, "They need to feed on human blood."

At dusk a wind began to blow from the south carrying an acrid dust which caught at the nostrils and stung the eyes. As the purple haze deepened to night the wind ceased to leave a dusty film over the town. One stirred by pedestrian boots into flurries which rose to settle in new configurations.

"A hell of a world." Angado turned from the window of the room they had hired. "And a hell of a deal Vargas gave us. How much did you pay him, Earl? Whatever it was it was too much. Turn thief," he sneered. "Join a bunch of suicidal hunters. Feed parasites. He had to be joking."

Dumarest made no comment, lying supine on one of the two narrow beds the room contained, looking at the cracked and stained ceiling. One typical of the rooming house with its sagging roof, creaking floors, dingy walls. At night parasites crawled out to feed.

"Earl?"

"He wasn't joking. We're taking his offer."

"I'd rather steal!"

"Then you do it alone." Dumarest sat upright and stared at the younger man. "Vargas will set it up for you if you pay. Find a location, arrange to dispose of the loot, even put you in touch with help if you need it. To him it's just a matter of business. To you it will be your life."

"If I'm caught."

"You'll be caught. People living on worlds like this have learned to take care of their property. And they aren't gentle with those who try to take it. Both hands amputated, blinding, hamstringing—most likely you'll be sold to the mines to work until you die. That needn't take long."

"But to feed parasites!"

"Most do it all their lives." Dumarest rose from the cot. "Maybe we can find the captain in a tavern; if not I'll go to the ship. But first we'll get something to eat."

The food was poor, as cheap as they could find, as everything they had eaten since leaving Lowtown had been cheap. As had the wine, the accommodation, yet still the money dwindled away. Cost was relative; what would keep a man a week in Lowtown would barely buy a snack on the plaza, yet to return to the sprawling slum was to commit suicide. Gengiz had had a brother who had sworn revenge.

Things Angado thought of as he spooned the redolent stew into his mouth. He wasn't hungry but Dumarest had insisted that he eat; good advice from a man who too often had never been sure when he would be able to eat again. A trait nurtured by poverty as were so many others and Angado wondered if he would ever be able to master the basic techniques of survival. Not the ability to maintain life in the wild, that was a matter of learning how to best use available resources, but to master this new and frightening environment. How would he have managed without Dumarest? His money would have been squandered, thrown away on gaudy trifles, on food which gave bulk but little nourishment, on high-priced comfort which, compared to his normal life style, would have been hardship.

It would have been better to have died as Perotto had intended. Perotto! At the thought his hand tightened on the spoon.

Dumarest, watching, said, "Relax. He can wait."

"Can you read my mind?"

Just his hands, his face, the lack of focus in his eyes. Signals he had learned to read when facing gamblers in the salons of a hundred ships. As he had learned to read other signals, more important, those worn by men intent on taking his life.

Tables or the arena. Money or blood. It was all the same.

Neary, the captain of the *Audran*, was a human wasp; thin, vicious, with a hatchet-face and cold, hostile eyes. He sat alone in a corner of a tavern close to the field, a bottle standing before him, a plate of flat cakes smeared with a sickly paste at his elbow.

To Dumarest he said, "I've been expecting you. Vargas said you might be along. Got the money?"

"We've money."

"Then sit. Have some wine. A cake." The captain hammered on the table and snapped at the girl who answered the summons. "Bring wine, girl. A flagon of your best for me and my friends." He looked at Dumarest. "He'll pay."

"Like hell he—" Angado fell silent as Dumarest gripped his arm.

"He'll what?" Neary had caught the objection. "You don't want to buy the wine? Is that it?" His head thrust forward like that of a snake. "Well?"

"I meant that I'll pay, not him." Angado swallowed his anger, realizing the mistake he'd made. One born of ignorance—never before had he needed to beg favors from a captain. "Get the wine, girl. A big flagon and your best."

It arrived as drums began to pulse and a dancer spun on the cleared space before the tables. One artificially young, paint masking her face, the lines meshing her eyes. Her body needed no artifice, mature, full-brested, hips and belly rotating in an age-old enticement. The clash of metal merged with the sonorous beat of the drum; coins hanging from her costume more suspended from her ears, her throat, her wrists and ankles. Twinkling discs which caught and reflected the light so as to bathe her in shimmering brilliance.

As she froze to a sudden, abrupt immobility at the end of her performance those watching yelled their appreciation and flung coins at her feet.

"Nice," said the captain, pouring the wine. "But I've seen better. On Elmer and Hakim especially. They start them young on those worlds." He drank and pursed his lips. "Did Vargas tell you what our cargo is?"

Dumarest nodded.

"They'll need feeding," said Neary. "If they don't they'll go comotose and sporifulate. If that happens they won't be worth the atoms used to move them. Lost profit always makes me angry. Need I say more?"

"I get the picture."

"And your friend?" Neary grunted as Angado nodded.

"Good enough. It'll cost you two hundred." He paused for a moment then added, "Each."

"We don't have to dodge the gate."

"So?"

"So we can afford to haggle." Dumarest reached for the flagon and poured all goblets full. "How many mikha are you carrying? A full load? I thought so. You know how much blood they're going to need? I see you do." He lifted his goblet. "Your health, Captain. Now let's start talking sense."

The drum began to pulse again as they left the tavern, the deal made, the wine finished. Angado staggered a little as he stepped into the open air; with Dumarest doing the talking he'd had nothing to do but sit and drink. Now he halted and stared at the field.

"Why not go aboard now, Earl? Neary wouldn't mind."

"We've things to do." Dumarest led the way back into town. "We need plasma," he explained. "It'll eke out our blood. Some frozen whole-blood too. We can get it at the infirmary."

"Why couldn't Neary?"

"He'd have to pay," said Dumarest, patiently. "This way he gets paid."

Together with free labor to handle the cargo. Angado smiled as he thought about it then lost the smile as he tripped and almost fell. Standing beside Dumarest, motionless, he heard a soft scrape of boots.

"Earl—"

"Be quiet!"

Dumarest had heard it too; the grate of soles on the grit deposited by the wind. It came again from a point behind and was echoed from a point ahead. The sounds of wayfarers making their way home or crewmen heading for the field and their vessels. But few roamed the streets of Yuanka at night and crewmen had no reason to creep through the darkness.

"Thieves," whispered Angado. "At least two of them. Waiting for us, Earl?"

If so they wouldn't wait for long and there would be more than two. Dumarest sniffed at the air and caught the scent of sweat and wine coupled with another, unmistakable odor.

The stink of Lowtown and, smelling it, he knew the danger they were in.

"Move." He touched Angado on the arm. "Slowly. Stagger and make noise. Pretend we're together. If anyone comes at you don't hesitate. Hit out and run."

Dumarest crossed the street as Angado began to sing, the noise covering the rasp of his own boots. Shadows swallowed him as, staggering, the younger man lurched down the street talking as if to a companion.

"Good wine, eh? And that dancer was really good. I'd like to know her better. Have her dance just for me." A pause then, "Why not? My money's good. I bet she'd agree if I asked. Damn it, Earl, let's go back and put it to the test. Five hundred. I'll give her five hundred if—" A rattle as Angado walked into a garbage can. "What the hell is that?" And then, louder, "Who the hell are you?"

They came running from either end of the street, four shadows which solidified into men. Shapes which carried lengths of pipe which whistled as they cut through the air.

As the bottle Angado had snatched from the garbage whistled to land with a soggy impact on the pale oval of a face.

Dumarest was running before he hit the ground, his hand moving, the knife it held giving it heft and weight, the pommel smashing against a temple to send a second attacker down. A third followed, screaming, hands clutching his groin and Dumarest turned to hear the gong-sound of beaten metal as the pipe the remaining man held slammed against the garbage can Angado had lifted to use as a shield. One blow and then the pipe fell and the man was running to vanish in the darkness.

"Come on!" Dumarest ran, halting as a whistle broke the silence, turning to head back in the opposite direction. "Quick!"

The four would not have been alone. Others would have been placed as lookouts, the whistle a signal from one of them. Hunting packs followed a pattern the same if animal or human. To surround, to run down, to attack, to kill and then to feed.

Dumarest slowed as he reached the mouth of an alley, speeded as he found it innocent, slowing again as he neared the end of the street. Another crossed it forming a junction restricting his choice to a right or left turn.

As the whistle came again from behind, louder, more imperious, he headed toward the left, Angado following.

To the men waiting with flashlights and guns and nets which caught them both like flies in a sticky web.

Chapter Ten

The cell was a box ten feet long, eight wide, eight high. One fitted with a double bunk and primitive facilities. The door was a barred grill, the window another. Through it Dumarest had seen the dawn come to lighten the sky, the blue shimmer as the *Audran* had headed into space. At noon a guard took them to an office.

It was as bleak as the cell, holding little more than chairs, a desk, the terminal of a computer. The official seated at the desk was old, tired, heavy lines marring the contours of his face.

"Be seated." Inspector Vernajean gestured at chairs. "I think this can be kept informal. But before we begin do either of you have any complaints as to how you have been treated?"

"No." Dumarest had a bruised cheek, Angado a cut lip and a welt on his forehead. "None at all."

"Good." Vernajean relaxed a little. The injuries could have been accidental but the older of the two had the sense not to make an issue of them. "Last night we received reports of prowlers in the Voe district of the city. A patrol was sent to investigate and you were apprehended. Apparently you were running from the scene of a crime. Other men were also seen but managed to elude arrest. Well?"

Dumarest said, "It was a coincidence."

"Explain."

"We were making our way from the field and heard someone cry out for help. There were too many for us to handle so we ran to get assistance. That's when you caught us."

"Can you describe the men?

"No, it was dark."

"How many were there?"

"About six."

"Four attacking two others?" Vernajean didn't wait for an answer. "In a way you were lucky to be caught. The patrol disturbed men who had been waiting for you. Scum of Lowtown who had broken curfew as had the others. Does the name Birkut mean anything to you?"

"I've seen him."

"And Yuli?"

"No."

"Gengiz's brother. He's sworn to kill you but you know that. He's taken over and maybe he's getting impatient. That attack could be repeated and the next time you needn't be so fortunate. You appreciate my position?"

Angado said, "We were attacked and had to fight for our lives and all you worry about is your position? How about doing your duty? If you know who was responsible then go after them and make them answer. Why are—"

"Shut up!" Dumarest didn't look at his companion. "He's young," he said to the inspector. "Still learning. He doesn't realize that Lowtown is what it is because you want it to be that way."

"What other way can it be?" Vernajean shrugged. "Men without money, without hope, growing more and more desperate. An abscess ready to burst and spread infection all over the city. It has to be drained."

By using men like Yuli to rule and bleed malcontents into the mines. A ready source of cheap labor for the installations which provided the wealth of the planet. But, for Yuli, the price of cooperation was the death of those who had killed his brother.

"The monks have spoken for you," said the inspector. "We have no wish to antagonize the Church but—" His gesture completed the sentence. "And there is another thing. Without a job or funds you are not allowed within the city during curfew. If you should be picked up by a patrol and found to be deficient then you can be fined or sentenced to the mines. I tell you this so as to make you aware of your position."

"Thank you," said Dumarest.

"Position?" Angado was less gracious. "What position? If

it hadn't been for your damned men we wouldn't be here now!"

"If it hadn't been for them we could be dead." Dumarest rose to his feet, facing the inspector. "Can we go now?"

"Yes. Your property will be returned at the desk outside." Vernajean rose in turn. "A last word to the pair of you—do not stay on Yuanka too long."

Outside Angado swore with savage bitterness.

"They robbed us! The bastards took half our cash!"

"But left half."

"We should complain. Go back and make a formal accusation."

Dumarest said, "You heard what the inspector said. He was warning us. Leave Yuanka or wind up in the mines or dead. Maybe some of those officers in there want to see us that way."

"So they robbed us to force us to the brink and over." Angado looked bleak. "How do we get out of this hell-hole? Steal? Gamble? Try our luck at the wheel? Put all of our money on a single turn?" His laugh was brittle. "What have we to lose?"

Everything, but that was the nature of a true gamble. To risk life itself on the throw of dice or the flip of a coin and yet, as Dumarest knew, the need to win was often the surest way to lose.

Yet there was more than one way to gamble.

The place had the familiarity of home; the smell, the sounds, the sight of the ring, the tiered seats, the cubicles in which men sat with blank faces or sported with artificial gaiety. The environs of the arena in which men faced each other with naked steel to maim and kill for the sake of gain.

The promoter was curt. "It's fifty for show, as much if he lasts five minutes, a hundred more if he wins." He looked at Dumarest standing black-faced, vacuous, a seeming moron. "Does he know what it's all about?"

"He knows." Angado, primed, acted the part of an entrepreneur eager for a profit, uncaring how he got it. A cynic who shrugged as he added, "You won't be disappointed. He's good and has scars to prove it. Fifty, you said?"

"When he's due to climb into the ring." The promoter

ignored the outstretched hand. "Gives you a chance to place your bet," he explained. "Of course, if your man doesn't make good, you do."

"Medicals?"

"We've a doctor but you pay his fees." The promoter glanced at his watch. "The prelims are all arranged; first and third blood stuff. Your man'll feed a main event."

"For fifty?"

"You can double it if you bet right." The promoter sharpened his tone. "You want it or not?"

"I'll take it." Angado obeyed Dumarest's signal. "Doubled, eh?"

"Sure, if he makes a good entry. That's settled then. He'll face a prime contender."

To be hacked, slashed, maimed and slaughtered to provide a bloody spectacle. Dumarest had seen such too often; men driven to the ring by desperation, unskilled, untrained, trusting to luck and the mercy of their opponents. Ending as things of carmined horror, dying to the frenzied yelling of the crowd.

Dumarest could hear them from where he sat, imagine their faces, avid, feral, features taut with sadistic pleasure. Men and women converted by their blood-lust into mindless, reactive beasts. Thrilling to the sight of blood, of pain, the stink of fear.

"Earl?" Angado had heard the shouts and seen some of the men coming from the ring. Youngsters, mostly, many with gaping wounds. Some having to be supported, others making their own way to where the doctor worked on a bench covered by a stained, plastic sheet. "Earl, are you sure you want to go through with this?"

"We've no choice."

"To hell with the money. We can work in the mines, try hunting, anything. This is butchery."

Sport seen from a different angle and he no longer felt the vicarious pleasure he had when seated in a place close to the ring. Enjoying the combat, the near misses, the cuts, the hits and scores, the deaths while comforted by the knowledge that he would remain unharmed.

Dumarest said, "Make sure the odds are right. I'll stumble when entering the ring, look vague, act stupid. Easy meat to anyone who knows his stuff. I might even take a cut. Give me a couple of minutes to decide then make the bets.''

"You're good," said Angado. "You have to be. And fast, I know that. But I still don't like it.''

"Do your part and I'll do mine.''

"Yes, but—'' Angado broke off as someone screamed from the medical bench. A hoarse, animal-like sound of sheer agony. "God!''

The scream came again, the doctor's voice rising above it, harsh, commanding.

"Help me, someone! Hold this man still! Hold him, damn you!''

Angado gripped sweat-slimed shoulders, fighting the explosion of muscles as he forced them back on the bench as others gripped threshing arms and legs. The man was young, face contorted with pain, intestines bulging through the slit abdomen. Blueish, greasy coils stained with blood and lymph, one slashed to show a gaping mouth.

"Keep him still!'' Air blasted as the doctor used a hypogun to drive anesthetic into the bloodstream directly through the skin. He'd aimed at the throat and the effect was immediate. As the patient slumped into merciful unconsciousness the doctor sewed the slashed intestine, coated it, sprayed it, thrust it and the others back into place. More sewing, spraying and sealing and the job was done. "Next?''

"Will he live?'' Angado lingered as a couple of porters carried the man away.

"He should.'' The doctor was middle-aged, hard, coldly proficient. "Thanks for your help. You running a contender?''

"Yes.''

"Tell him not to be heroic. It's better to drop and grandstand than to end up cut all to hell. Cheaper too.'' The doctor raised his voice. "Who's next?''

A man with a slashed face, an eye gone, the nose and lips slit. He was followed by another clutching at the ripped fabric of his shorts, thick streams of blood running between his fingers and staining his thighs. A third had a small hole on his torso and coughed and spat blood from a punctured lung.

A winner—in the clash and flurry of edged and pointed steel the one who stayed longest on his feet gained the prize. But even winners could be hurt.

Angado moved back to Dumarest, his façade cracking, sweat dewing his face. The smells were making him gag and the cold indifference of others to pain made him feel alien and vulnerable. In this madness Dumarest was a consolation. A rock of security.

One who seemed asleep.

He leaned back against the wall, muscles relaxed, eyes closed, his breathing deep and even. A man devoid of tension, sitting easily, resting so as to conserve his energy. To Angado it seemed incredible, then he realized that Dumarest was not asleep at all but had deliberately thrown himself into a trance-like state of detachment. One which suited the pose he had adopted, that of a moronic intelligence unable to imagine the consequences of failure and willing to be guided by a sharper mind.

"It won't be long now." The promoter paused, taking time during the interval to check on the next events. Known contenders were safe enough but ring-fodder sometimes grew apprehensive and needed encouragement. "I've picked an easy one—old, slow, too gentle for his own good. Abo hates to see a man hurt. A fault, but one in your favor." He glanced at Dumarest. "He need anything? A pill, maybe?"

"I can handle it."

"See that you do." The promoter jerked his head as a roar came from the crowd. Naked women, fighting with clubs, had given rise to yelled appreciation. "Better get him ready."

He bustled away and Dumarest rose, stretching. As always he felt the tension, the anticipation which crawled over his skin like multi-legged insects. Warnings of danger which even the shower could not wash away. Cleaned, oiled to prevent a grasping hand gaining a hold, he donned shorts and reached for his knife.

"Not that one!" An attendant called from where he stood before the passage leading to the ring. "We provide the weapons. Hurry up if you're ready!"

Sound exploded from the crowd as they reached the passage, a shrill, yammering roar which caused the partition to quiver.

"That was a killing!" The attendant sucked in his cheeks. "The crowd always like to see a man go down. Right. You're next!"

"The money." Angado was insistent. "I get paid or he doesn't show."

"It's here." The attendant handed over the cash. "Happy now?" He didn't bother to hide his contempt. "Damned leech!" Then, to Dumarest, "Right, friend. Off you go."

To the head of the passage, the open space, the watching crowd, the ring, the man who waited to kill him.

Dumarest tripped as he entered the auditorium, clumsy as he climbed into the ring to stand beneath the glare of overhead lights, the knife they had given him hanging loosely in his hand. One an inch longer than his own, not as well honed, not as well balanced, but the ten inches of edged and pointed metal could do its job. It glittered as it caught and reflected the light, a flash which caught the eye and attention of a woman in the third row. One aging beneath her paint, her costume designed to accentuate her charms. The jewels she wore were no harder than her eyes.

"That man," she said. "What do you know about him?"

"Nothing." Her companion was indifferent. "Just fodder for the ring. Forget him."

A thing not easy for her to do. Narrowly she watched as Dumarest moved, noting his build, the scars, the lean suppleness of his body. A man who was more than he seemed to be and her own experience doubted his artifice. Too often she had acted the innocent in order to gain an advantage and such maneuvers were not restricted to women.

"A thousand," she said. "I want to back him for a thousand."

"To win?"

"Please don't be tiresome. Just do as I ask."

"No." He was definite. "It would be a waste of money. Abo isn't due to go down yet. Another few bouts and then, when his reputation is at its peak, the odds will be right for a killing."

"You could make one now. That man will win."

"He won't be given the chance." The man ended all argument. "Here's Abo now."

He bounced into the ring, the idol of the crowd, a winner who seemed set to go on winning. He smiled with a flash of white teeth, brown skin oiled, glistening beneath the lights.

The tight mat of his hair was thick against his skull, the arms long, corded with muscle. He moved like a cat, restless, poised and balanced on the balls of his feet. An animal, fast, quick, dangerous, he basked in the shouted adulation of women, their screamed invitations.

Promises of their beds and bodies if he would only kill . . . kill . . . kill!

And kill he would despite the rules which stated that a man down should be left alone and given the chance to yield.

"Attention!" The voice over the speakers was flat, emotionless. "A fight to the finish between the defender Abo and the challenger Earl. To your corners." A pause during which tension mounted. "Ready?" Another long, dragging wait then, like a cracking whip, "Go!"

And the third man entered the ring.

He was always there, always waiting, an invisible shape dressed in sere habiliments with bony hands ready to collect his due. Death who could never be avoided, now present by invitation.

A presence Dumarest ignored as he did the crowd, the lights, the ring itself. They blurred into a background framing the object of his concentration. The tall, lithe, man before him. One armed with a knife. One intending to kill.

And the killing would not be merciful.

Dumarest could tell it from the sadistic grin, the stance, the feline movements, the twitch of the eyes. A man playing cat and mouse in order to please the crowd. Eager to give them what they wanted; blood, pain, fear, the long-drawn agony of the final end.

A man who knew he could deliver. Success had augmented his natural skill; easy kills rubbing away the edges of hesitation. Now he moved slowly forward, blade extended before him, point out, edge upward, light glinting from the honed steel. His free hand made inviting gestures.

"Come closer," he said. "A shallow cut and you go down. Scream a little and writhe as if you're in pain and then it's over. Easy money for a scratch. Why make it hard, eh?"

Dumarest said, "I've got to last five minutes. I need the fifty."

"A cut you go down, get up and hit my blade. Plenty of noise and movement. Then another little cut and down you go again, this time to stay. A good deal, eh?'' The purring voice hardened a little. "Take it while you've got the chance."

A gamble in more ways than one. A cut would enhance the odds against him and so up the take, but Abo could cut too deep; to trust him would be suicide. A risk Dumarest would never normally have taken but the man wanted to gain popularity, a quick and easy win would work against that and, to cooperate now, would be to gain a later advantage.

"Right," he said. "But be careful."

They closed, blades flashing, ringing, darting like the tongues of serpents, Dumarest saw the lance of Abo's knife, its slashing, backhand sweep, and moved sideways away from its edge as it sliced into his side. A shallow gash barely more than a scratch and far less serious than Abo had intended. Dumarest clapped his free hand over the wound, masking it, enhancing the flow of blood with the pressure of his fingers. Staggering, he retreated to a halt, gasping, at the far side of the ring.

A pretense to gain time, to allow Angado to place his bets, but looking at Abo he knew he had made a mistake.

The man had more than luck and skill to help him win.

Knives were not always what they seemed. A blade could have inbuilt weaknesses and snap under pressure. Or the hilt could be hollowed to contain various vapors which could be spurted through holes in the guard. Abo's blade held indentations which held a numbing paste.

Dumarest cursed his stupidity but he was trapped in a game over which he had no control. There had been no chance to examine the weapons. None to take elementary precautions and, had he fought to avoid being cut, the odds would have fallen too low.

Now only speed could save him.

He met Abo's rush with a flick of his hand, the blood it had held flying to spatter on the smiling face, the cruel eyes. An attack followed by his own rush and the air shook to the thin, harsh ring of steel, the crowd roaring as Dumarest sent his blade home in a vicious slash which would have spilled Abo's guts had he not twisted to take the edge on his hip.

A cut followed by another, a third, deep gashes which laced the torso and marred the smooth brown skin with a patina of blood.

Backing, Abo fought back. He was quick, skillful, alert now to the real danger. The smile gone now, replaced by a snarl as he turned into an animal fighting for its life. Matching the one Dumarest had already become.

Time became meaningless, the universe itself diminishing to a matter of cuts, parries, dodges, feints, thrusts, attacks, ripostes. As life became a matter of crippling cuts, weakening blood loss, of speed and instinctive action unhampered by the slowing need for thought.

Abo lunged, missed, received a slash which crippled his left arm. Spinning, he brought up his edge, the blade halting as Dumarest blocked the motion with the barrier of his forearm against the other's wrist. A moment of strain then they parted, Dumarest seeing his target, aiming for it against the growing numbness.

Feeling the jar of metal against bone as a sun burst in his eyes.

It was a flare of light so intense as to be a physical pain and Dumarest stepped backward, hands lifted, feeling the ice-burn as steel cut into his body. A blow repeated as he moved blindly to one side and he tasted blood in his mouth and the pain as metal scraped over bone. A thrust which had penetrated a lung, another searing into his bowels, a third tearing at his liver in a storm of edge and point to send him down.

To lie blinking on the floor of the ring as vague images replaced the blackness—the lights, a shadow standing tall against them, one smeared with blood, grinning in the rictus of impending death, but still standing, still upright.

Abo enjoying his victory.

"Earl!" Angado was at his side. "You're hurt! How badly— God!" His voice rose as he called for help. "Get him to the doctor! Fast!"

Dumarest sagged in the rough hands which grasped and carried him. Pain was something not to be ignored, an agony which filled every crevice of his being. The pain and the knowledge that, at last, he had reached the end.

It happened and, in the arena, it could happen to anyone at any time. A slip, a moment of carelessness, a touch of overconfidence and, when least expected, death would reach out its waiting hand. He had seen it happen to others and now it had happened to him. The luck which had served him for so long had at last run out.

"Earl!" Angado was pleading. "For God's sake—Earl!"

A voice like a whisper in the darkness echoed by others, one stronger than the rest.

". . . internal injuries and there is profuse hemorrhaging . . . needs extensive medical care but it'll be costly . . . cryogenic sac . . . move to the institute . . . need to waste no . . . must hurry . . . hurry . . . hurry . . ."

The doctor pronouncing the sentence of death, his voice becoming ragged, lost in the encroaching gloom. Death by inaction. Death from reasons of poverty. Death because he couldn't pay for the treatment necessary. Death, smiling wider now as he always smiled, coming closer . . . closer. . . .

"No!" Dumarest forced open his eyes fired by the spark deep inside of him, the urge to survive which gave him a transitory strength. Darkness still clouded his vision and obscured shapes but one, close to his face, had to be Angado.

"Earl! Those bastards fired a strobe-laser into your eyes. There was almost a riot from the crowd. All bets are off."

Which is why he was lying on the bench with the doctor treating him with basic remedies. Stanching wounds and killing pain while knowing he could only stave off the inevitable.

"My arm!" Dumarest lifted his left forearm. "Get a banker-machine. Money, you understand? I've money."

". . . hang on and and maybe I can get something arranged. A loan or—"

"Money!" Dumarest snarled in impatient anger. "Listen to me! Get a banking machine and do what's necessary. Do it." He sank back, blood welling to gurgle in his throat, to drown him with his life's fluid. To spray in a carmine fountain as he coughed and spat and said, while he was able, "I've money, damn you! Credit! Use it and . . ." He felt himself beginning to fall into an eternal oblivion. "Angado—I'm relying on you!"

Then there was nothing but the endless spinning tunnel of darkness and, at the end, the single point of a glowing star.

Chapter Eleven

Avro screamed; a shout which illuminated the shadows of his sleeping mind. A challenge hurled at the wind, the sky, the male hovering before him on spread wings. An aggressor, young, ambitious, fired by the biological need to perpetuate his genes. One screaming his intent as Avro screamed his warning but knowing, even as he screamed, that this time it wouldn't be enough. And to strike first was half the victory.

Wind gusted around him as he launched himself from the peak with a thrum of wings. Pinions which threshed the air as he fought to gain height, to turn, to hurl himself at the challenger, arms extended, fingers spread, feet lifted to deal a devastating kick. One which missed as the other twirled aside, to kick in turn, to register a blow which sent Avro spinning.

Whirling as he was attacked again with feet and hands, toes and fingers ripping at his wings, adding to the strain they already fought to overcome.

The penalty of age when the body grew too gross and the great pectorals, the deltoids, began to weaken. A time when lift was slower, agility less, vulnerability a growing menace.

The moment of truth for an angel who refused to yield his nest, his women, his position in the community.

A thing Avro knew from the instinct buried in the body and brain of the host he dominated as he knew that to fold his wings and fall would be to signal his peaceful withdrawal from the conflict. An act which would save his life and leave him to fly alone as long as his wings would carry him. To join the flock of other aging males who had been forced to yield to younger blood. Tolerated and even cared for as long as they recognized the victor's right.

But Avro was too new to this body and its way of life. Too entranced by the novelty of emotion and conditioned by the subtle knowledge that, for him, death in this body would not mean extinction. So he fought until the blood ran from a dozen wounds and his wings were in tatters. Fighting on until he began to fall, to continue to fall despite his struggles, wheeling in circles to the rocks below, the wheeling becoming a tumble, a drop, a sickening plunge to the jagged teeth waiting to smash out his life.

An impact which was the hammer-blow of extinction, filling his eyes with a flash of vivid light.

One which lingered as he jerked upright on his bed to sit, fighting for air, hands clasped over his eyes.

"Master!" Byrne calling from beyond the door attracted by his screaming. Concerned by it also; it was becoming too frequent. "Master?"

"All is well." Avro lowered his hands. "Enter."

He stood upright as the acolyte came into the room his face masked, hands steady. The chamber was as it had been when he'd retired for the sleep which should have refreshed him but had not. And the pressure at the back of his skull seemed to have grown worse.

To the aide he said, "You have something to report?"

"Nothing positive, Master."

"Have the electroencephalograph scans arrived from the ship?"

"They are on your desk, Master."

"That will be all."

"Yes, Master."

Avro stared after the aide as Byrne bowed and made his way through the door. Insubordination was out of the question: an aide was trained to obey, but obedience could be tinged with more than a desire to please. Had his use of the title been all it seemed? Normally to address a cyber as "Master" was a recognition of superiority and an admission of dependency but overuse could make its own point. One of accusation or even of contempt. Had Byrne, by what could be regarded as zealous courtesy, shown his disquiet?

He was a spy, of course, as Tupou was a spy, as all

acolytes were spies. Eyes and ears to see and listen and a mouth to report. Had he told Ishaq of the screaming? Had the cyber reported the incidents to Central Intelligence? Had he received secret orders in turn to watch and assess and, if necessary, to restrain his nominal superior?

Avro lifted his hands and pressed them against the back of his skull. Why had Marle ordered Ishaq to join him? Why had rapport altered so strangely? Why did he so constantly dream of his life as an angel?

What was happening to him?

Part of the answer was in the electroencephalograph scans sent from the ship.

Seated at the desk Avro studied them, checking one against the other with quick efficiency. The variations were minor but unmistakable and when combined with other records from other examinations left no doubt. Even so he double-checked before leaning back to stare at the tinted panes of the window.

They were diamond-shaped, made of various hues, the sunlight streaming through them forming a tessellation of mauve, orange, red, blue, emerald which flowed over the floor, the desk, the scattered papers on the surface. A transient beauty which Avro ignored as he stared at the window, the sun, the endless expanse of the dried sea bed beneath it. On it men and machines crawled in a constant search for nodules of manganese and other valuable minerals. The only source of wealth on the world and one controlled by a combine who had reason to be generous to the Cyclan.

Janda, a world as hostile as Velor, was set in the mathematical center of a sphere in which Dumarest would be found if he was still alive.

Closing his eyes Avro saw it again; the open grave, the metallic sheen which broke into rippling motion, the fretted bone revealed as the insects scuttled from their feeding place. Dumarest or some other? How to be sure?

Yet on the answer depended his life.

Avro glanced at the scans, again conscious of the pressure within his skull. One not born of imagination but of harsh reality. The Homochon elements grafted within his brain showed unmistakable signs of change. Normally quiescent until stimulated by the Samatachazi formulae they lay incorporated in the cranial tissue; a sub-species of reactive life akin to a beneficent growth which enhanced telephathic contact and made rapport possible. Now, those within his brain were growing.

Swelling like a bomb which would rip his skull wide open.

He would be dead long before that could happen and insane long before he was dead. His only hope was to have his brain removed from its bony casing and placed in a vat forming part of Central Intelligence. There the Homochon elements could grow as they normally did once the transfer had been made and his intelligence would not be affected. But, to gain the final reward, he must redeem his past failure and capture Dumarest.

Find him, capture him and deliver him to Marle. And do it before it was too late.

Angado said, "Home, Earl. Lychen where I was born. Now I'm back I wondered why I ever left."

He wore soft fabrics touched with vibrant color; reds overlaid with green trimmed with gold piping. A costume which once had suited the lanquid dilettante he had been but which now no longer belonged to the lean body and hard face. Something he spotted in the reflection carried by the window before which he stood and he turned, smiling, arms lifted in a gesture of greeting.

"Cousin! How wonderful to see you! In truth there were times when I thought we should never meet again. I was desolate as I am sure you would have been at the concept. Have you wine? A comfit? Something to ease the endless burden of this tiresome round?" His arms fell, his tone hardening as he looked at Dumarest. "Well?"

"Is that how you used to talk?"

"To Perotto and his cronies? At times, yes. It amused me to see their contempt."

"Is that all?"

"No," admitted Angado. "The spoiled sons of rich families tend to act the fool until it is no longer acting. To go into raptures over a trifle, to swear vengeance on a slight, to vow undying feality to a friend—" He shook his head in disgust. "How little they know of real values. You've taught me a lot, Earl."

Dumarest said, dryly, "I hope enough for you to stay alive."

"I'll be careful." Angado spun in an elaborate pirouette. "A fool left Lychen and a fool has returned. One concerned about his finances and for no other reason. He'll be apologetic, gracious, swearing it's all a mistake and promising retribution— but I'll remember Yuanka."

"And remember a man can smile and murder as he smiles."

"I shan't forget." Angado hesitated then said, "There's a lot I shan't forget, Earl. I—"

"You don't owe me."

"I can't agree. If it hadn't been for you I'd be stuck on Yuanka."

"If it hadn't been for you I'd be dead." Dumarest rose from the deep chair in which he'd been sitting. "We each helped the other. The slate's clean."

"But your money!"

"What good is money to a dead man?"

Dumarest moved from the chair and crossed the room to stand as Angado had done before the window. It gave on a wild and rugged scene; bleak rocks, cracks, slimed stone the whole dominated by the sheet of water which dropped from above so close it seemed it could be touched. A waterfall of stupendous proportions falling to the floor of the chasm far below. Mist filled the crevice, hiding the upthrust teeth of stone with shifting rainbows, clouds of drifting spume. The roar of the impact was the deep, prolonged note of an organ.

One muted by the treble glazing, absorbent padding, the very shape of the rocks molded with cunning skill to reflect and minimize the noise.

"My grandfather built this, Earl." Angado had come to stand at Dumarest's side, his voice quiet, brooding. "I think he wanted to leave his mark and chose to build a challenge against nature itself. Beauty turned on beauty to enhance the total effect. At times, standing on the balcony, I've felt what he must have done. The utter insignificance of a man when compared to the universe. How futile all our striving seems. We're like rats fighting to garner corn we'll never be able to eat. Denying others for the sake of greed and, in the end, what does it all amount to?"

Dumarest said, "How many know that I'm here?"

"Does it matter?"

"How many?"

"A few. Servants, of course, and some others. Those of the ship would have talked and to deny your existence would have been stupid. You're a friend. Someone I met while traveling." Angado's eyes were direct. "In my circles it is considered impolite to be too curious about such associations. You'll be safe here, Earl."

"Why do you say that?"

"You talked. Back on Yuanka when you'd been sedated prior to treatment you said enough for me to know you were looking for something and something was looking for you. My guess is you're afraid of the Cyclan." Angado paused then, when Dumarest made no comment, added, "It's your business, Earl, but as I said you're safe here. Just eat and sleep and laze around and leave the worrying to me."

"Thanks."

"Forget it. We're friends, aren't we?" Angado frowned as he noticed the time. "It's getting late and I don't want to offend my hostess. Wynne is a wonderful person but can be too punctilious at times. I'd like to take you with me, Earl, but it's better left for another time. I can learn more from her if we're alone."

"She might think the same."

"She might," Angado agreed. "But I'm no longer the man she used to know."

He left with a lift of his arm, smiling, his step light as if already he was fitting into his part. One which might delude those who had known him if they didn't look too close. Alone Dumarest roamed the apartment. It was large, a collection of rooms adorned with various works of art; carved blocks of crystal, vases shaped in erotic patterns, tapestries depicting scenes of bizarre fantasy. Decoration reflecting the imagination of the man who had built a cave in the side of a cliff simply to stare at a moving sheet of water.

Seen from the balcony it was awesome.

Dumarest felt the wind of its passing, the moisture from it which dewed his face, heard the deep, sonorous note from its impact against the rocks far below. A hypnotic sound as the water itself held a dangerous attraction. The fall seemed static; a curtain made of shimmering crystal, adorned with

ransient gleams of reflected light. Beauty which masked the
power of it, the crushing, destroying force born of relentless
gravitation.

Leaning against the rail Dumarest looked below. A master-
mason had cut away the rock to leave the balcony suspended
over the chasm and he stared at the roiling mist rising from
the depths. At night the mist was illuminated with colored
glows but was now a mass of white and gray, twisting,
turning, rising like innumerable fountains. Hands which reached
and arms which invited and he felt the attraction of it, the
urge to throw himself over the rail into its embrace.

An impulse he resisted, stepping back to lean his shoulders
against the wall as he looked upward at the summit of the
fall. No rock had been allowed to remain to break the smooth
outward curve, one enhanced by skilled adaptation, and Dumarest
appreciated the artistry behind the concept. Here was nature
as it should be, complete, perfect, a living example of a poem
or a piece of music. Art in its purest form with all irritations
carefully erased. An ideal—nature was not and could never
be like that. As no life could be all harmony. As no death
could be a gentle release.

Dumarest had met death too often; the small death when he
had ridden Low, lying doped, frozen and ninety percent
dead in caskets designed for the transportation of beasts.
Risking the fifteen percent death rate for the sake of cheap
travel. Another kind of death, more traumatic, when the
host-bodies he had occupied when using the affinity-twin had
ceased to exist. Real, physical death softened only by the
knowledge that it was only the body which was dying and not
himself. Yet the pain had been real, the fear, the helpless
terror of an organism that struggled to survive.

And he had met death beneath Abo's knife.

A death as real as any he would ever know for the agony
had been present, the bleak realization of final extinction, the
oblivion into which he had fallen. A darkness which had
encompassed the universe and no death, no matter how exotic,
could do more. Only the prelude could be extended but when
death came, it came, and for him it had come on a small
world in a dirty ring circled by avid, hungry faces eager for
the spectacle he provided.

But did the dead ever dream?

Looking at the waterfall Dumarest remembered the dream he had had, or had it been a vision? A sea as wide and vast as any ocean could ever be. A sun which had drawn vapor from it, to condense into droplets, to fall as scattered rain on hills and plains and mountains. To be lifted again, to fall, to end in rivers which returned to the sea. A cycle repeated endlessly for all time.

Did the ocean care what happened to its substance? Did the drop of rain know from where it had come and to where it must go?

Was conscious life nothing but a temporary awareness of individuality?

A shadow touched Dumarest and he felt a sudden chill, one vanishing as the cloud which had covered the sun moved on beneath the pressure of wind. An incident which broke his introspection and he straightened with a sudden resolve. There had been too much thought of dying—now he needed to find life.

And it was time to look for the person on Lychen he most wanted to find.

An elevator rose from the apartment to the upper surface, one circled by spiral stairs which he used for the sake of exercise. A long climb which sapped at his weakened reserves and Dumarest sat on a bench as he surveyed the area. To one side sprawled a hotel holiday complex; something of recent construction that, he guessed, would never have been allowed by Angado's grandfather. Lawns surrounded it dotted with flower beds set in a riot of vivid colors. A long observation walk reached out over the head of the falls invisible from below. The body of massive timbers supported a mesh of lighter beams forming a protective barrier. Flags surmounting the structure streamed in the wind.

A breeze which carried a fluttering scrap of paper to rest against his boot.

"Please, sir, may I have my drawing?"

She was about eleven, tall, well-made, with strong white teeth showing between generous lips. A girl now solemn though the hazel eyes held the hint of laughter, her round face stamped with determination. She wore a long striped dress bound with a wide sash at the waist, the ends falling on her left side to a point below the knee. In her left hand she held a sketching pad and a sheaf of pens.

"My drawing, please."

"May I look at it?" Dumarest stooped to grasp it, holding it until she nodded. "Did you do this all by yourself?"

"Yes."

It was an animal, brightly colored as no real beast could ever be; the body red, the snout green, the tail blue to match the paws. A creature of fantasy yet in true proportion, the colors blending to form a pleasing whole.

"That's Ven," she said. "He's a sort of mole but I like Ert better, he's a bear."

Dumarest looked at the pad she held out for his inspection. Again the creature was colored in bright hues and was standing upright like a man. Another creature of fantasy and, like the first, it bore the stamp of a real talent.

"May I?" Taking the pad he turned the sheets, pausing as he saw a round, pitted, silver disc. One in close proximity to a circle bearing a cross, A drawing which could have depicted a moon—and the crossed circle was a symbol of Earth. "Did you think of this all by yourself?"

"Of course. I intend to be an artist when I grow up and an artist must be able to compose a picture."

"I'm sorry." Dumarest forced himself to be casual. "I meant did you see these designs anywhere? In an old book, perhaps? A painting?" Hope died as she shook her head. "Are you sure?"

"We haven't any old books. Mummy says they smell. Grandfather has some but he keeps them locked away." She held out her hand. "May I have my pad now, please."

"Of course." Dumarest closed it and looked at the cover. "No name?"

"Of course I have a name. Everyone has a name. I am Claire Jane Harbottle. My pad, please." Taking it she said, "You don't look well. You should walk around and get the air. My nanny says it is very healthy on the platform. Good-bye, now."

She ran off with a rustle of fabric, a girl oddly demure in formal garments, yet full of life and vitality. She would make her mark if her talent was allowed to flower and, if nothing else, she had given him good advice.

Dumarest rose and wandered between the flower beds as he followed a sweeping path which would bring him back to the observation platform. The wind stung his eyes, gusting, the flags streaming to fall and hang in limp abandon, to flutter again in varied hues, to droop and hang again. An odd pattern for such a place and Dumarest wondered at the vagery. A thought swallowed by another of far greater importance.

Had the girl merely dreamed up the notion of a pitted sphere and a circle barred by a cross or had she actually seen them somewhere? A decoration of a nursery wall, a painting, an illustration in a book—something seen and forgotten to rise to the forefront of her mind when triggered by the need of artistic expression. If so her grandfather could be of help—but would Lychen hold two people who could solve his problem? Did both know how to find Earth?

A stone turned beneath his foot and he stumbled, catching his balance, annoyed at his lack of attention. He had wandered among a collection of statues, tall figures simply clad and wearing haughty and disdainful expressions. Some had been adorned with flowers, others with cruder additions many displaying a ribald sense of humor. They fell behind as Dumarest lengthened his stride and headed toward the platform. If the girl was still around he wanted to learn more from her. Or from the person she would be with.

He heard the scream as he reached the foot of the ramp, a high shriek followed by words.

"Claire! Come back, Claire! For God's sake, child, come back!"

Wind had caught a picture, wafting it to catch against an upper timber and with grim determination she was going after it. Dumarest saw the small shape climbing doggedly up the framework, to grab at the paper, to miss as it blew to a farther point. To grab again as the flags stirred and wind blasted in a sudden gust.

One which thrust at the exposed shape, catching the striped dress, billowing it, using it as a sail to push the small figure off its perch.

To send it toppling from the framework into the air, the sweep of the waterfall, the long drop to the rocks below.

Dumarest moved as the woman screamed again, this time in horror, not warning. He stooped, hand lifting weighted with his knife, eyes judging time and distance, the movement of the sash over the timbers. His arm swept in a wide circle, steel glittering as it left his hand, thudding broadwise through the sash and into the wood beneath. A spike which held her suspended, twisting in the wind which caught her hair, her dress, the sash around her waist. Before it could slip free Dumarest had the girl cradled in his arms.

Chapter Twelve

Edelman Pryor was seventy years old and looked it. He wore drab garments and walked with a shuffle but still had a sharp mind and intelligence. His home matched the man, old, decaying, full of dust and forgotten corners yet retaining a staid dignity—demonstrated by the decanter, the wine, the courtesy with which it was served.

"Your health!" He lifted his glass to Dumarest. "And my thanks for what you did. If I had money you could take it all. The girl is precious to me." He sipped and added, "We are not related in blood, you understand, but she is kind enough to call me her grandfather. When young she used to stay here with her mother."

"Her father?"

"At the time was busy on other worlds. Now he is home where he belongs. Why didn't you want him to know what happened?"

"Would it help if he did?"

"No. He would give you his thanks and anything you might ask but—"

"It would be a memory he can do without." Dumarest tasted his wine not surprised to find it thin and acid. "The governess will say nothing for her own protection and the girl is wise beyond her years. Even her mother needn't be told."

"The dress?"

"Only the sash was damaged. An accident." Dumarest shrugged. "To the young such things happen all the time."

But the incident had been of value, giving him an introduction to the old man, one arranged by the governess who had been too relieved to argue. Now, sitting in the dim chamber, sipping the weak and acid wine, Dumarest waited for the courtesies to end.

"You're a friend of young Angado," said Pryor. "I heard of his return. I hope for his sake he has learned caution during his travels. Are you close?"

"We traveled together."

"And are staying with him?" Pryor sipped his wine as Dumarest nodded. "Well, he could do worse. And your own reason for coming to Lychen?" He blinked when he heard it. "An interest in antiquities? Books, maps, old logs? What appeal could such things have for a man like you?"

"The same as they have for yourself." Dumarest set down his glass. "I learned something today and saw items of interest. A drawing of a moon and a symbol I recognized. Things which could have been seen here in your house. Perhaps in the books you keep locked away."

"From a curious little child who was into everything she saw." Pryor chuckled and finished his wine. "There's no mystery about it. I collected the books for a client and the things you mention could be found within them. One at least held symbols and pictures and charts of some kind. I must confess they held little appeal but they did represent a profit. As did the maps and logs and other items I bought for later resale. As a dealer, you understand, specializing in the abstruse and rare. In fact one of my acquisitions is to be seen in the museum; a plaque inscribed with what must be a hymn of praise to an ancient god. One called Apollo. You have heard the name?"

"No."

"A pity." Pryor was disappointed. "I loaned it to the museum for the duration of my life but I expect it'll stay there for as long as they want it. Or until someone is willing to pay the demanded price. But if you are really interested in ancient things then I may have something which could interest you." Rising, he went to a corner and rummaged in a cabinet, returning with an object in his hand. "Here."

It was squat, grotesque, a female figure with swollen belly and huge, sagging breasts. The face was blurred, the nose a rounded knob, the eyes deep-set pits of blankness. Three inches high the depiction was wholly engrossed with female sexual attributes.

"I've had it for most of my life," said Pryor. "It's very old and must have been an object of veneration at one time. Some say it is a fertility symbol but I'm certain it must be more than that. The representation is that of the mother-figure and so could have associations with the very source of human life. If so it is an ideal depicted in stone. Primitive, crude, but unmistakable."

And to him of high value—why else should he have kept it so long? Dumarest studied the figurine, sensing the raw power of it. A woman. A mother. A female born to breed. Naked, unashamed of the attributes which made her what she was. The epitome of every male consumed with the desire to gain the only immortality he could ever know—the children which would carry his genes.

"Erce," whispered Pryor. "Once a man told me she was called Erce."

Mother Earth, a name Dumarest had heard before. One appropriate to the figure; turned, it would be Earth Mother.

Earth Mother?

"The man who told me that told me more," Pryor reached for his glass, found it empty, refilled it with a hand which created small chimes from the impact of the decanter with the rim. A quiver which sent ripples over the surface of the wine. "It's nonsense, of course, as anyone can see, but an interesting concept in its way. You may have heard of it. Some profess to believe that all life originated on one planet. All the divergent races on one small world. Logic is against it. The numbers are of no importance, natural increase would account for that, but how to account for the diversity of color? How, under one sun, could people be white, black, brown, yellow and all the shades between? They would be affected by the same climatic conditions, the same radiation, water, air, food. How to account for the different germ plasm?" He drank and wiped droplets from his lips. "As I said it's just an interesting concept. The image itself yields a certain tactile pleasure which you may enjoy. The story, of course, is nothing. An exercise in logic, you might say. No intelligent man would give it a moment's credence."

And only a fool would have mentioned something he took such pains to deny.

Pryor was old but no fool and the figure meant more to him

than he admitted despite his protestations. A gift for a service rendered, the most he could offer, and yet one it hurt to lose. The talk had been a cover for his emotions, the code by which he lived enforcing the gift as a matter of honor. As it would regard rejection as an insult. Dumarest must accept it or make an enemy and, on Lychen, he had only one friend.

Quietly he said, "I am honored. I have seen an object like this once before. On a far world in a commune of those who claimed a common heritage and held a belief close to that you spoke of. They call themselves the Original People." He saw the clenching of a thin hand, the sudden spatter of spilled wine. Without pause he continued, "To them the figure was sacred. They kept it in a shrine."

"So?"

"I think it a pleasant custom." The hand and the spilled wine had been enough but if Pryor knew of the Original People or subscribed to their beliefs the secrecy shrouding them would block his tongue. A thing Dumarest knew and accepted. "I receive this figure from you as a valued gift," he said. "But gifts should be shared and I return it into your keeping. To be guarded until such time as I choose to send for it. It is agreed?"

"I don't understand." Pryor frowned, cheeks flushing with a dawning anger. "Are you refusing—"

"No!" Dumarest was sharp. "That is the last thing I intend. Let me explain. The plaque in the museum is yours, agreed? They are displaying it for you. Safeguarding it. I am asking that you do the same with my figure. I have reason for the request which I am sure you will appreciate." His voice deepened, took on the echo of drums as he said, "From terror they fled to find new places on which to expiate their sins. Only when cleansed will the race of Man be again united."

The creed of the Original People and Pryor gulped, his eyes startled, veiling as he stared at Dumarest's enigmatic face.

"I see," he said. "I—yes, we understand each other. It will be an honor to do as you ask. But I feel at a loss. It is not right that you should leave this house without some token of my appreciation." Pryor gestured with a thin hand. "Look around. Choose. Anything you wish will be yours."

"This." Dumarest rose and picked up his wine. "I choose

what this glass contains." He drank and added, "The wine—and the name of the man for whom you collected old books."

It was late when Dumarest returned to Angado's cavelike home and the apartment was deserted aside from servants who remained discreetly invisible. One answered his summons, a man who stood with quiet deference, eyes widening as Dumarest asked his question.

"A study, sir?"

"Something like that. A room with books and maps. Surely there are maps?"

"I can't be certain, sir. There was a clearance when the old owner died and the present master has been long absent. Also changes have been made." A lift of his hands emphasized his inability to be precise. "But if maps are present, sir, they could be in the desk."

"And that is where?"

In a room barren of windows lit by lamps shielded by decorated plates of tinted transparency. One with a soft carpet on the floor and erotic paintings on the ceiling to match those writhing on the walls. A library of a kind but one which would have held a bed rather than books. Now it held neither—just a chair, a display cabinet holding small artifacts, a desk which dominated the room with its massively carved and ornamented bulk. The top remained closed beneath Dumarest's hands, the maps it may have contained beyond his reach.

A small irritation and one he ignored as he returned to the main salon and stood before the wide window watching the play of colored illumination streaming upward from the mist at the foot of the waterfall. In it the curtain of water became an artist's palette alive with vibrant hues; reds and greens, blues, oranges, dusty browns and limpid violets, shards of gold and streamers of silver, changing, blending, forming transient images which dissolved as soon as recognized. A magic reflected by the rock wall facing him across the chasm, the stone taking on a strangely disturbing aspect as if the stubborn material had softened and become the door to new and alien dimensions.

From behind him a woman said, "It's beautiful, isn't it, Earl?"

She was tall, slim, wide shoulders adding to the hint of

masculinity accentuated by the close-cropped silver hair which framed a broad face and deep-set eyes of vivid blue. A woman who moved with a boyish grace, no longer a girl, the maturity of near middle-age giving her a calm assurance. Her mouth, wide, the upper lip thin, curved into a smile, revealed neat and even teeth. She wore a masculine garb of pants and blouse, her femininity displayed in the fine weave, the intricate pattern of complex embroidery. Her voice was deep, resonant and Dumarest thought of the sound of fuming water.

"My lady?"

"So formal," she said. "So cautiously polite. Lhank said you were that."

"Lhank?"

"Lord Hedren Angado Nossak Karroum. When there are so many names it helps to use initials." Her laughter rose in genuine amusement. "Don't look so startled. I have a key, see?" She lifted it swinging from her fingers. "You were busy when I arrived. What did you think of the den? Lhank Five had some peculiar attributes and had a liking for the bizarre. Lhank Six was something of a prude and Lhank Seven—well, you know about him."

"And nothing about you."

"Nothing? He didn't mention me? His old and trusted friend?" Again her laughter drowned the murmur of the waterfall. "Wynne Tewson. At times I like to think that he left Lychen because of unrequited love. Now he has returned and with a new friend. A hero." Her eyes narrowed, became appraising. "There are many who will envy him."

Dumarest said, "The key you have in your hand—will it fit the desk?"

"What?" She frowned as he explained. "The desk in the den? What the hell is it doing there? Now if it was a bed maybe we could use it. Did you know that as the lights change color the paintings take on new and various forms? Speed the illumination and you get a kind of stroboscopic effect; one minute the walls are full of coupling shapes, the next a crowd of goggling voyeurs. Old Lhank certainly had imagination."

"The desk?"

"Is just that, a desk. Put in the den to get it out of the way. I can't open it but even if I could it holds nothing of value.

Why are you so interested." She blinked as he told her.
"Maps? You are interested in maps?"

"Just of this area. This world. I like to know where I am."

"Yes," she said. "That I can imagine. But there are other
ways to find out aside from maps. How about a personally
conducted tour? I've a raft waiting and we could take a ride.
Go to the Steaming Hills or look at the Pearls of Toria. If
you're really interested in old maps we could even pay a visit
to Chenault."

The name Pryor had given him, the same as that Shakira
had mentioned back in the circus of Chen Wei. The man
Dumarest needed to find—but without leaving a trail others
could follow.

Casually he said, "Is that why you are here? To take me
on a conducted tour?"

"No. I came to bring you a message. Lhank wants you to
join him."

"Do you always do what Angado wants?"

"Angado?" She smiled with a secret amusement. "Is that
what you call him? How touching. Such a sweet name."

"He chose it."

"Of course. He would. His mentor called him that when
he was young. The monk—did he tell you about Brother
Lyndom? He had a great influence on his charge and it would
have been better for Angado to have joined the Church. That
or the Cyclan, but he lacked the application for that. For
either, if the truth be known, an inherent weakness of
character—why else should he have run away? Would you
have done it, Earl? Given up the leadership of a great House
and gone roving?"

"Perhaps, if the reason were strong enough."

"Such as?"

Dumarest said, meeting her eyes, "Unrequited love?"

"No!" She was emphatic in her denial. "Never that!
You'd abduct the girl, fight for her, rape her, even, but never
leave her."

"I was talking about love," he said. "Not lust."

"And love is sacrifice? Is that what you mean?" She
thought about it for a moment then said, "You should be
right. Maybe I misjudged Angado. Certainly he seems differ-

ent now, more adult, more confident. He tries to hide it but it's there."

She had noticed, had others? Dumarest said, "He wants me to join him, you said. Why and where?"

"To give him moral courage, perhaps." The small mounds of her breasts lifted beneath her blouse as she shrugged. "Or to show you off to his friends—the hero with whom he battled against incredible odds and managed to survive. Give it a week and it will be you whose life he saved. Give it another and the whole thing will be forgotten. No novelty lasts long on Lychen." Her eyes moved past him to settle on the shifting lights beyond the window. "Boredom, Earl. Why are we always so bored?"

"You know the answer to that."

"Too idle, too rich, too spoiled. The cure?"

"You know the answer to that too."

"Work. Fill every minute of every hour with unremittent effort. But what if you can't work? Or don't want to work? Or there is no work to do?"

Dumarest said, "Some people are fat. They are fat because they eat too much. It's as simple as that."

"And we're bored because we're lazy—it's as simple as that. Or is it?"

"Lazy," said Dumarest. "Or afraid. No matter what reason you choose to blame, the cure lies within yourself."

"As it does with those who are too fat." She looked down at her slender figure. "Would you like me if I were fat, Earl? Great bulges here and here and here." Her hands moved to breasts, belly and buttocks. "Masses of flesh, quivering, bouncing, sagging, grotesque. The thought is disgusting. I'll never grow fat." She sucked in her stomach the action making her even more like a man. "Let's get out of here."

"To where?"

"Didn't I tell you? To the party, of course. But first we take a ride."

The raft was a work of art, small, gilded, the controls and body shielded by a transparent canopy which could be rolled back into the sides of the vehicle. Wynne handled it with skillful ease, rising with a velocity which sent air gusting in a muted roar as the hotel complex beside the head of the waterfall fell away to become a model touched with silver light.

"Scared?" Turning she shouted above the wind. "Or do you like the taste of danger?"

"No."

"No what? You're not scared or—"

"I don't like the taste of danger and, yes, I am scared." His hands closed on her own, his strength mastering hers as he adjusted the controls. The raft slowed in its climb, steadied, began to drift toward the east. "If you're trying to prove something you've made your point."

"Which was?"

"To show me how well you can handle a raft, perhaps." His hands moved a little and she gasped as the vehicle veered and, suddenly, began to fall. As it leveled Dumarest added, "We can both handle a raft."

"And we both can be scared."

"Which makes us human."

"And honest." She looked at him, starlight touching her hair, adding a sheen to its silver smoothness so that from where he sat she seemed to be haloed in a nacreous luminescence. "Are you honest, Earl?"

"As much as you, my lady."

"My name is Wynne. I would like you to use it." As he remained silent she said, "Please."

"Wynne." He smiled as he repeated the name. "Wynne. I would guess, my lady, that the name is appropriate."

"Don't be so damned formal!"

"Am I right?"

"Yes, I guess you are." She smiled in turn, the quick anger forgotten. "I usually get what I want in the end." She looked over the edge of the raft at the waterfall to one side and far below. "Spoiled," she said. "Old Lhank must have been mad to have tried to improve on nature. It's too smooth, too pretty. Like a painted harlot skilled in deception." Her eyes moved to Dumarest as if inviting comment then, as he remained silent, she said, "To hell with it. Let's find something more amusing."

The raft lifted with a sudden savage velocity, darting forward to throw Dumarest back, wind blasting at his face and hair. In it the woman's silver crop took on a life of its own, each hair seeming to stand out with individual vibrancy. A fuzz which dominated her face, enlarging her head so that, for a moment, she seemed grotesque.

Then, as she touched a control, the transparent canopy rose to a halfway position, forming a windscreen which protected them from the blast. Above the droning, organlike note from above, her laughter rose high, brittle-edged.

"Do you like it, Earl?"

A child enamored by a toy and demanding praise. He studied her profile in the starlight, recognizing her willfulness, her need to hold attention.

"Earl?"

"A souped-up raft," he said. "I've seen them before. Helped clear away their wreckage too. Overstrain the antigrav units and they can fail. Sometimes the generator can fuse. There are better ways to commit suicide."

"Old man's advice," she sneered. "You're too young to give it and I'm too young to take it. Hold on!"

The speed increased, auxiliary burners flaring to add their thrust, turning the raft into a rocket which lanced on a tail of flame across the sky. One which ended over the loom of hills shrouded in luminous smoke.

"The Steaming Hills," she said. The canopy lowered and Dumarest caught the scent of acrid vapors. "By day they look like bones hiding in drifting mists. At sunset and dawn the mist becomes a sea of blazing hues, but at night the trapped energies are released and they are what you see now."

A place of enchantment and drifting glows. Light and shadow in which bizarre shapes took form to change and vanish and reappear in a different guise. A moving, living chiaroscuro of incredible complexity and stunning beauty.

"There is a game the courageous sometimes play," she said. "Couples take their rafts to a certain height then cut lift and make love. The trick is to finish before the raft hits the ground." Her eyes were brooding as she stared at the luminous smoke. "Sometimes I think that those who don't return are the lucky ones."

Dumarest said nothing but moved closer to the controls.

"Think of it," she breathed. "The rush, the urgency, the race against time—all sauce to add piquancy to the experience.

Have you ever done anything like that, Earl? Would you dare to try?"

"No."

"Why not? Afraid? Or don't I appeal to you enough?" She faced him, eyes direct as they searched his own. "Would you be willing if I were other than what I am? Bloated? Broad hipped? A breeding machine for children? Or would you rather—"

"No!" he said again, his tone sharp. "Leave it at that."

"But—"

"Love isn't something to be timed. If it's worth having at all then, while it lasts, time has no meaning. And I'm too old to play childish games."

"And too young to need such stimulation." She smiled and reached for the controls. "Let me show you the Pearls of Toria."

They stretched across the plain round lakes of limpid brightness, a cluster which formed a giant necklace of pendants and ropes edged with a soft vegetation and gentle banks. The result of an ancient meteor strike which had created a host of isolated aquatic worlds.

Landing, Wynne jumped from the raft and ran to the edge of a pool shot with streaks of varied color. Stripping, she stood naked, slim, lithe, a column of nacreous whiteness, then dived into the pool to leave a widening circle of ripples.

Before they reached the shore Dumarest had joined her.

The water was cool, refreshing, the luminous trails made by darting fish disturbing drifting organisms. Tiny motes which blazed with light to the impact of larger bodies. Like an eel the woman twisted, swam, glided through the water to touch him, to dart away, to return with extended hands. A game in which he joined feeling the smooth sleekness of her, the muscle beneath the skin, the hard, tautness of her body.

One which lay beside him when, exhausted, they had climbed on the bank to sprawl on the sweet scented grass.

"Earl!"

He turned to look at her, seeing the silver sheen of her hair, the direct stare of her eyes, the message they held. One repeated by her body as she moved, small breasts signaling her femininity, narrow hips and waist belying it, the slender column of her thights parting to leave no doubt as to her sex and her need.

"Earl! Earl, for God's sake!"

Then she was on him, straddling him, engulfing him, lips seeking his, closing on them, teeth nibbling as her nails raked his flesh. Moving with a fevered determination to drain him and, her own need satisfied, to slump against him.

"A man," she murmured. "My God, but you're a man!"

She caressed him until again time ceased to have meaning and she lay against him warm and sleek, the silver crop of her hair against his shoulder, the nails of her fingers scratching like kitten claws over his torso.

"Happy, Earl?"

"You've made me so."

"That's nice." She snuggled closer to him then, turning over, looked at the stars. "I hate them, Earl. All those bright points. Those suns with all those worlds. Every time I look at them I'm reminded of the fact I'm a failure. Scared to move away from the familiar into the strange. Living a more and more constricted life. . . . At least Angado had guts. He took a chance and—" She turned her head to look at Dumarest. "No," she said. "He didn't take much of a chance. Paid to stay away—for him it was just a holiday. But he came back and he brought you with him. For that I thank him if for nothing else."

"I thank him too."

"For me?"

"Yes, Wynne." Dumarest made the name sound like music. "For you."

"Darling!"

In the pool a fish jumped in mating frenzy, the trail of its passage a golden streak of flame.

Chapter Thirteen

The party was dying and Angado was bored. A condition he shared with others but while their ennui was a cultivated pose or the genuine result of too few things done too often his was the product of comparison. Spall prating about the hardships of poverty—after experiencing Lowtown his complaints were both trivial and ridiculous. Plaskit and his talk of personal combat—a man who would never dare risk his skin against an armed opponent. Or even an unarmed one; his talk was based on long-distance viewing and the safe slaughter of helpless game. Crixus who spoiled the air with words appertaining to the idealistic existence to be found when living close to nature in the wild. Deakin Epstein, Spencer—all fools unconscious of their folly; posturing, gesticulating, making sly allusions, asking pointed questions.

The women were as bad, each in their own way acting a part, jealous, spiteful, vicious even as they made overt invitations. Angado remembered Dumarest's advice about those who could smile and murder as they smiled. The majority, no, they lacked the elemental courage. Some, perhaps, driven by whim or the pursuit of novelty. Only a few fitted the bill and of them all Perotto was the most ruthless.

"See how our young friend fits so easily back into his niche, Juan? Almost it seems as if he has never left us."

At his side Juan Larsen, sycophant, aide, a living echo of his master, nodded and smiled with thin lips. His tone was as acid as his words.

"Men are like the birds, Luigi. Some find the strength to leave the nest of their own volition. Others have to be helped. Some need to come crawling back to the only haven they can find. A pity. The Seventh Lord of the Karroum would, I thought, have had more pride.''

Angado shrugged, remembering the part he was playing, the pose he needed to maintain.

''Pride and hunger make poor bedfellows, Juan. Blame my return on the accountant who forgot to continue my agreed allowance.''

''He will have cause to regret it for years to come.'' Perotto turned to his friend. ''You were a little hard, Juan. Angado has not had an easy time. In fact he was lucky to survive at all. A fascinating story, you must hear it soon, but one now we can put behind us. In any case it would be enhanced by the presence of his friend. One who still has not arrived, I see.''

''Earl will be here soon. I sent Wynne to bring him.''

''Wynne?'' Perotto raised his eyebrows. ''Wynne—ah, I see. A fine woman and she would have made you a good consort. A good wife too, once she had proven her ability to continue the Karroum line. Maybe that was your trouble, Angado. A man should not live alone. A woman at your side would have eased both body and mind.''

''Or driven him insane.'' Larsen was blunt. ''Not all men share your taste, Luigi.''

''True, but who is to condemn? One likes cake another bread and who is to say which is right? But the head of a House has obligations and—well, never mind that now. Wynne, you say?''

''Yes, Wynne Tewson.'' As always Perotto made him feel small, inferior, and Angado fought to maintain his calmness. A battle partly lost as he snapped, ''You know damned well who she is.''

''Who and what,'' said Perotto. ''It is obvious why your friend is so late in joining us. You made a bad choice of messenger, Angado. You should have sent another to pick up your friend. By now they are probably over the Steaming Hills or sporting in the Pearls of Toria. Not that it matters. We must be tolerant of such things. To be otherwise is to act the barbarian.'' Smiling he added, ''And to be jealous is to act the fool. Don't give your friends the pleasure of seeing your discomfiture.''

''You are mistaken.''

"Of course. I often am." Perotto turned and signaled to a servant bearing a tray laden with goblets. The wine was smooth, subtle in its hidden potency, but Angado gulped it as if it had been water. Watching him Perotto said, "I think it time for our surprise, Juan. Will you fetch the box?"

As Larsen turned and walked away Angado said, "Box?"

"Merely a container for something rare and rather strange. The product of a new confectioner who has set up business on Schenker. A trader brought me a sample and you may find his wares amusing." Perotto took the box Larsen had fetched. "That will be all, Juan."

Angado reached for more wine as Perotto lifted the container. One made of finely carved wood inset with a tracery of metal and stone, gold and silver merging with emerald, ruby, amethyst, sapphire, amber, the clear sparkle of diamond, the somber hue of opal. The lid opened beneath his touch to reveal a compartmented tray filled with small mounds of rich darkness decorated with a dusting of minute pellets of a thousand hues.

"Chocolate." Angado was disappointed. The wine had made his head spin a little; boredom had sent him to the anodyne of alcohol too often during the evening. Now he looked at his cousin. "Ordinary chocolates."

"Far from that, Angado. Once tasted they can never be forgotten. For a discerning palate the effect is incredible. Here!" Perotto touched a chocolate with the tip of a finger. "Try this one."

"Aren't they all the same?"

"Far from it. Each contains within itself an entire new world of titillation. In fact I can't resist their promise." Perotto lifted the chocolate he had urged Angado to take, placed it within his mouth, closed his lips and sighed with audible satisfaction. "Magnificent!"

He had eaten and it would be safe to do likewise and courtesy demanded the acceptance of the gift. Angado picked a chocolate, placed it within his mouth, bit down and was suffused with a sudden plethora of flavors. There was peach and apple and chard and a touch of grize and a hint of orange and the tang of grape and of embra and lemon and . . . and . . . and . . .

And a sharp, overwhelming thirst.

His goblet was empty but the servant was already making his way toward him. The wine accentuated rather than washed away the flavors, joining with them to tease his palate and to wake memories of the recent experience. One amost duplicated as he ate another sweet. Almost—as Perotto had said there were differences and now he tasted blood and leather and the sweat from hides and horn and more subtle exudations from a hundred living things. Tastes which aroused strange stirrings and sent his hand again to the refilled goblet, the goblet to his mouth, the wine to his stomach.

Close to him a woman laughed with a thin, vicious chittering.

"Drink deep, Lord Karroum, it will help you to bear your loss. But don't worry, your friend will return."

"Unless Wynne kills him."

"A good sleep and he'll be as good as new and think of the fun you'll have scolding him."

More laughter and more wine to drown the sound and another chocolate and still more wine. And more laughter and too many grinning faces and walls that moved and air that stank.

And a floor that rose to hit him in the face to the sound of ribald cheers.

Dumarest heard the noise as the raft settled to land, the yelling incorporating a name which sent him jumping over the side and into the rooom before Wynne had time to kill the engine. Angado lay where he had fallen, face down on the carpet, a ring of shouting partygoers laughing and deriding his condition. They scattered as Dumarest burst through them to stoop over the fallen man.

"Don't worry about him, Earl." A tall, young, languid man smiled as he reached out to touch Dumarest's arm. "I may call you that? It's much better to be on friendly terms, don't you think? I'm Yip Zaremba—you can call me Yip. Or anything you like as long as it's nice. But don't worry about your friend. He's just drunk too much. Once he's sober he'll be all over you unless—"

He staggered back, blood dripping from his lips as Dumarest lashed the back of his hand against the simpering mouth. To Wynne who had joined him he snapped, "Get some water. Salt too. Hurry!"

"Earl—"

"Do it!"

Angado sagged in his arms as Dumarest lifted him, bending him over a table which he swept clear with a brush of his arm. A woman screamed as he snatched feathers from her ornate headdress then fell silent, watching as Dumarest forced open Angado's mouth with the fingers of his left hand, standing behind and beside him as he was thrust the bunch of feathers down the exposed throat.

"Earl?" Wynne had returned with a jug of water and a container of salt. "Shall I mix them?"

He nodded, busy with the feathers, feeling the limp body in his arms begin to jerk and heave. A moment then vomit sprayed from Angado's mouth to spatter the table with regurgitated wine, food, blobs of nameless substance.

"Now!"

Wynne poured as Dumarest kept open the mouth, wiping it clean with his hand before bending Angado over again, using the feathers as before, again causing the limp man to empty his stomach in a liquid gout.

"More."

"Earl, is it—"

"More!"

Angado struggled as the water entered his mouth, pushing at Dumarest with weak hands, barely aware but conscious of his discomfort. As Wynne emptied the jug Perotto came through the crowd to watch as Dumarest clamped his arms around the young man, jerking to constrict the stomach, again flooding the table with a now almost clear fluid.

"What's going on here? What are you doing? If the man is ill a doctor should be summoned. This conduct is inexcusable."

"He was drunk." Zaremba thrust himself forward, caked blood on his mouth. "I went to help and this boor struck me. A matter of jealousy it seems. I—" He broke off, backing as Dumarest turned toward him. "That is, I mean, well, they seem to be friends."

"Of course!" Perotto beamed, extending his hands in a gesture of welcome. "You must be Earl. I should have recognized you from Angado's description. Still taking care of him, I see."

"Someone has to."

"And you are best suited for the task. We must talk, you and I. Later perhaps? Before you leave?"

Dumarest nodded and led Angado to the windows, the cool air outside. A fountain cast a crystal shower into the air, droplets illuminated with subtle glows, mist that flowed as if made of silk. Light that showed the area deserted, sound that masked his voice.

"All right, what happened?" Dumarest frowned as he listened. "Chocolates?"

"They were harmless. Perotto ate one before my very eyes."

"One?"

"Yes, just the one." Angado frowned, thinking. "It didn't seem to make him thirsty but when I ate one I had to gulp down some wine. The same with the others but the one he ate didn't affect him at all." His face took on a deeper pallor as he realized the implication. "Poison?"

"I doubt it. Just something to get you drunk but all kinds of accidents can happen to a man who can barely stand. Or perhaps he merely wanted to make you look a fool. Lord Hedren Angado Nossak Karroum the Seventh—crawling and puking on the floor. Who would respect you after that?"

"Who will now?"

Dumarest said, "You were ill. A blockage in the windpipe or a constriction of the epiglottis—there is no need to go into detail. You've had it before and I recognized the signs. How did you get on with Perotto?"

"What?" Angado blinked, then shrugged. "He put the blame on a clerk. The allowance will be resumed together with that owing and with an increase. He was most apologetic and promised it will never happen again."

"Do you believe him?" Then, as Angado hesitated, Dumarest added, "You were reported dead. Did he explain that?"

"Of course. A message from the *Thorn*. He had it all to hand, Earl. The answer to every question I might ask. Once, I would have swallowed every word but not now. I've learned to be mistrustful." Angado gave a wry smile. "It seems I've still a lot to learn."

"We all make mistakes."

"I make too many. You warned me but still I acted the fool." Angado swayed and would have fallen had not Dumarest caught his arm. "Those damned chocolates," he muttered. "Earl!"

"Drink water and bring it up." Dumarest half-lifted Angado to the fountain. "Wash out your stomach. Quick now!" He watched as the other obeyed. 'Better?"

"I feel awful."

"Sick?"

"Queasy and my head aches like hell. That's just what I feel like."

And looked. Dumarest studied the pale face, the sweat dewing cheeks and forehead, the color of the eyes. Any poison would have been eliminated unless it was a subtle variety which had passed immediately into the bloodstream. A possibility but one he discounted; the death of Angado must not be too obvious.

"Get home," he said. "Get to bed. Call medical aid. The hotel should have a resident doctor. Can you manage on your own?"

"If I have to. Why can't you come with me?"

"I've an appointment to keep," said Dumarest. "With Perotto."

He sat in a room which echoed his dignity; a chamber rich in leather, wood, intricate carving and expensive fabrics. The chair behind the wide desk was like a throne and he occupied it as if he were a king. One who lifted a hand in regal greeting as Dumarest stepped toward him.

"Earl, be seated." Light blazed from the gemmed ring he wore as he gestured toward a chair. "My apologies for having kept you waiting but some affairs cannot wait. The penalty of duty, you understand. To be the head of the House of Karroum demands the sacrifice of all personal inclinations."

"A sacrifice you are willing to make," said Dumarest, adding, as he saw the other frown, "as Angado was not."

"He was too young. He is still too young and I am not talking of chronological years. His mind is unable to accept the concept of total dedication. The need to sublimate all private needs and desires for the sake of the greater good. Words." Perotto gestured, the light again blazing from his ring, one Dumarest studied as the hand was lowered. "How little they mean. Dedication, devotion, duty—labels, some

would say, for outmoded concepts, yet without them what of
the House of Karroum?"

"Ruin," said Dumarest. "Devastation."

"For the House and all connected with it. Entire families
made destitute because of a youthful whim or brash inex-
perience. I do not intend that to happen."

"There are ways to prevent it."

"Many ways," agreed Perotto. "What is Angado to you?"

"A friend."

"And?"

Dumarest said flatly, "I'm broke. Stranded here on Lychen
and totally dependent on Angado's charity. If he should turn
against me or fall sick or die I'd be sleeping in the fields and
living on dirt. That's why I acted as I did out there; my
concern was to keep him alive. Once I get a stake he can
sweat in his own juice. I wasn't born to be a servant."

"The price of friendship," murmured Perotto. "The price
of two High passages? Three?"

"To do what?"

"To persuade Angado to leave this world and never to
return. I've made him an offer—you can see that he accepts
it."

"Three High passages." Dumarest looked at the room, the
rich furnishings, the items of price. "A low price for what
you have here. Five would still be low but a little more
attractive. Paid in advance?"

"In your hand when you board. Of course there could be
more if your powers of persuasion are too strong to resist.
Fifty times as much if you can convince me Angado will
never return to Lychen."

"Fifty?" Dumarest pursed his lips in a soundless whistle.
"My Lord, you are generous."

"But hard to convince."

"You shall have positive proof. My word on it." Dumarest
rose from his chair. "Now I must see how my friend is
faring. A sick man needs a break from routine and there are
other worlds aside from those in the Burdinnion. Interesting
worlds, some a little dangerous, perhaps, but what is life
without risk?"

Perotto said, "How will you travel?"

"To the waterfall? Wynne will take me."

"She has already taken Angado. I'll arrange for a raft."
Perotto reached for an intercom then withdrew his hand as he
changed his mind. "No. I'll take you myself. Work has made
me stuffy and it'll be a chance to clear my head."

Outside dawn had broken, the day brightening as the raft
moved east. Perotto sat beside Dumarest, the driver a hunched
and silent figure at the controls. The air was clear, deserted
aside from minute flecks wheeling over the top of the waterfall:
birds scavenging the hotel complex, many settling to perch on
the rails of the observation platform. Close to the entrance to
Angado's home Wynne's raft lay empty on the grass.

She met them as the elevator sighed to a halt, turning to
lead the way into the main salon. The door to the balcony
was open, cool air wafting into the chamber together with the
deep organ-note from the chasm, until it died to a muted
drone as she closed the portal.

"Angado sat out there for a while," she explained. "I
tried to get him to eat but he wasn't hungry so I made him
take a shower and go to bed. The last time I looked in on him
he seemed to be asleep."

"How is he?" Perotto sounded genuinely concerned.

"As well as can be expected."

"I've been thinking of what must have happened. Some
fools at the party must have slipped drugs into his wine. A
combination which caused a syndromic shock. Maybe it was
triggered by the confections he ate. A special blend of exotic
flavors that I thought would amuse him." Perotto shook his
head in self-reproach. "I should have remembered his deli-
cate stomach. Even as a child he had to be careful of what he
ate. I blame myself for what happened."

"It wasn't your fault." Wynne glanced at Dumarest. "Do
you want to see him?"

"Not if he's sleeping."

"He might be awake. I'll check." She left the room to
return, shaking her head. "Still asleep and I guess it's best to
leave him that way. One thing, Earl, I managed to find the
key to that desk. You know? The one in the den. It's open
now if you want to check what's inside."

Perotto frowned. "Desk?"

"Earl wanted to examine some old maps. The kind of
thing Chenault is so fond of." Smiling she added, looking at

Dumarest, "I never did get to take you to him—well, we didn't have the time. Tomorrow, perhaps. If you find anything interesting he'll be able to explain it to you."

"The den," said Dumarest. "You know, I've forgotten where it is."

"Just down the hall and—" Wynne broke off, shaking her head. "How could you have forgotten so soon?"

"Maybe I've had other things on my mind." His eyes held hers, their message plain. "Come with me. You can show me that trick with the lights you mentioned. Perhaps I could learn something."

"I doubt it." Her smile was inviting. "Come on, then. I won't be long, Luigi, when I come back I'll make some tisane. You like tisane, Earl?"

"I'd like anything you make."

He followed her from the salon, a man eager to get her alone, to recapture the experience of the night, its joy and pleasure. Coming close to her as she paused before a door ending a passage, his left hand rising to rest against her back, his head lowering to touch her cheek with his lips.

As she relaxed he jerked open the door with his right hand, pushed with his left, slamming the door after her as she staggered through the opening. A second and he heard the thud of her falling body.

"Wynne?" Perotto called out as Dumarest neared the salon. "Wynne, is everything all right?"

He was standing beside the wide window facing the waterfall. He was not alone.

Chapter Fourteen

As a man Avro had never known physical pleasure. The operation performed on him when young had seen to that; one deft stroke of the scalpel had turned him into a living, thinking, unfeeling machine. But now he rode the crest of a giddy intoxication born of mental achievement.

Dumarest caught, trapped, safe in his hand.

The man the Cyclan had hunted for so long and who had escaped so often, leaving dead cybers to mark his success, now the living proof of his own efficiency. The key to his own survival; soon now he would be safe in his vat joined in a gestalt of his own kind.

A moment he relished, extending it as he saw Dumarest catch the scarlet of his robe, spinning, halting the movement of his hand toward the knife in his boot, lifting it instead to his chin. A casual gesture of outward calm to mask the tension within and a warning of the true nature of the man. One who had assessed the situation in a flash, recognizing the futility of violence, gaining time by talking while apparently relaxed.

"Cyber Avro. This is a surprise. I never thought to see you again."

"Did you think the Cyclan so foolish as to believe the report of your death?"

"It was worth the chance."

"Negated once you used your credited funds."

"Of course." Dumarest touched his left forearm with the fingers of his right hand. Watching as eyes followed the gesture, dropping the hand slowly to his side. "You learned I was on Yuanka and traced me from there. And found an ally,

I see. A willing accomplice. What is his price? The death of his cousin?''

Perotto said, "Where is Wynne?''

"Enjoying the sleep she meant for me. Your idea or hers? Or did you set the trap?'' Dumarest looked at the cyber. "My guess is that you were the guiding mind.''

"You knew.'' Perotto gnawed at the subject like a dog with a bone. "About the gas. But how?''

Small items adding to form an uneasy whole, the sum triggering the instinctive reaction of a man determined to survive. A shallow answer and Avro knew there had to be more; the trait he was certain Dumarest possessed and which gave him the thing known as luck.

Dumarest said, "She was too friendly on too short an acquaintance and too eager to show me the sights. Time gained for you to feed Angado that filth. Not just something to make him puking drunk; such sights must be common in this society. Nor to show his friends what a weakling he is; they already knew that. You wanted to arouse their disgust and win their sympathy. Left alone he would have vomited then climbed to his feet. He would have stunk and staggered and he would have had an overwhelming desire to talk. He would have babbled and revealed his innermost nature. Become maudlin, sentimental, affectionate, amorous—and we both know he has a dislike of women.''

"That is no secret.''

"As Zaremba demonstrated when he tried to stop me helping Angado. He knew you wanted him shamed.''

"That bothers you?'' Perotto sneered. "You? A common traveler? A sycophant? A criminal? A man willing to take money to kill a friend who trusts him? Do you deny that?''

"A trap to get the man wanting him dead into admitting it,'' said Dumarest. "You want him dead. That's why you're helping the Cyclan. That's why you used Cranmer.'' He looked through the window at the waterfall. "He almost got away with it.''

"He was a fool.''

"Just as you are. As any man is who works with the Cyclan. Do you imagine you can use them and then forget them? And what of your own danger? How can they allow you to live now you know so much? Soon you will begin to wonder why I am so important to them. What makes me so valuable." Dumarest paused then added, "Side with me and I'll tell you."

Information which could kill; had killed for the existence of the affinity-twin must not be divulged. Perotto was as good as dead and Avro could appreciate the skill Dumarest was displaying. Attempting to drive a wedge between himself and the other; dividing so as to rule.

He said, "You waste your time. Killing me will gain you nothing. The apartment is sealed and men are stationed outside. As an intelligent man you can recognize the inevitable and yield. Do not force me to use this." Avro lifted his hand and displayed the weapon he had kept hidden in his wide sleeve. One which would vent a cloud of stunning vapor at the pressure of his finger.

Perotto said, "He is armed. His knife—"

"Leave it." Avro knew of Dumarest's speed. "If he reaches for it I will fire."

To stun and render unconscious but not to kill. He was too important to the Cyclan for that, which meant Perotto would not be armed with conventional weapons; Avro could never trust his aim. An advantage Dumarest assessed as, again, he rubbed thoughtfully at his chin. The cyber was making the basic mistake of talking when he should have acted. A need to mentally gloat, perhaps, but a weakness which had yielded information as to the trap he had closed on his victim.

One from which he had to escape or die.

Dumarest moved to one side, away from the door at his rear, checking distance and opportunity. Perotto faced him on one side, Avro, gun leveled, stood before him and the window. Ready now to shoot or summon help—and once he fired and the gas took effect the thing would be over.

"I yield," said Dumarest quickly. "You are correct—I have no choice. There is no need to use the gas. It would be inefficient. I'd have to be carried and the elevator is small. It would be better if I walked. It would give you greater credit; my capture would be yours alone."

The truth and Avro knew it. The reason he had insisted on facing Dumarest leaving Ishaq and his men on the surface. A matter of pride if not of perfect judgment but what could go wrong?

His vision blurred as, suddenly, a pain filled his skull. Pain and the realization of the mistake he had made.

Now! He must correct it while there was still time. Now! The gun aimed as he fought a rising nausea, finger tightening on the release. Now!

"No!" The voice filled the chamber as Angado threw himself into the room. "No!"

He had waited outside, listening, an ally in reserve, now acting with speed which emulated Dumarest's own. A small, round tray left his hand, spinning across the room to strike Avro's wrist and send the vapor-gun to the floor. The cyber followed it, twitching, hands clutching at his head. Then Angado was close to Dumarest, stooping, snatching the knife from his boot, lunging toward Perotto with the blade lifted to strike.

"You lied to me. Cheated me. Wanted me shamed. You filth! You stinking filth! Die, you bastard!"

Words instead of action and time given for Perotto to spring to one side, to lift the hand adorned with the heavy ring, for something to spurt from it and land with a thin, waspish drone against Angado's skull.

As he fell Dumarest was moving.

He dived forward, low, rising as Perotto turned toward him, shoulder catching the underside of the hand aimed at his face and throwing it upward as he struck. One blow smashed into Perotto's stomach and sent him doubling forward. Another dropped him to the ground. A third sent him to sprawl, gasping, face upward as Dumarest fell to his knees beside him. As the ringed hand swung toward him he grabbed it, aimed the ring at the orifice of the gaping mouth, squeezed to release the darts held within the gemmed casing.

Two of them sang as they buried themselves deep into the soft inner tissue of the throat, creating a black crater of destruction, filling the body with toxic poisons as it filled the mouth with blood and pain.

"Earl!"

Angado was dying. The dart which had struck his head was buried deep above the left eye, already into the bone, the brain beneath. Dumarest knelt beside him, reaching for the throat, resting his fingers against the carotids.

"Earl! I—"

"Easy." Dumarest's voice was warmly reassuring. "Just relax, Angado. This is just a dream. A bad dream. When you wake you'll forget all about it. It's just a dream."

"No." Angado swallowed and then, incredibly, managed to smile. "It's real and I know it. As I want you to know something, Earl. I love . . . I ∴ . ." He writhed beneath Dumarest's hands, sweat dewing his face, his throat. "You, Earl. I love . . ."

He stiffened and lost the smile as he lost the power of speech and the one became the rictus of death as the other grew into a silence which filled the world. One broken by the muted drone of the waterfall, the faint, insectlike scrap of a moving hand.

Avro reaching for his gun.

It lay beneath the wide window and his fingers touched it as Dumarest reared upright, closed on it as he moved forward, twisted it to aim as he approached, fired as, holding his breath, he dived toward the door.

Opening it as green vapor closed around him, falling through it into the open air of the balcony, clutching the rail as the wind tore the clinging mist from his face and body and his lungs burned with the need for oxygen.

Seconds dragging into minutes then he breathed and breathed again of the cool, damp, life-giving air.

Avro lay slumped on the floor, his breathing shallow, his gaunt face relaxed in the sleep the gas had created. A man felled in the moment of victory by the pain which had turned his mind and body into a rebellious mechine. Dumarest checked he was helpless then snatching up his knife returned to the balcony and hung dangerously over the rail.

Beneath him the rock had been cut away in a smooth concave sweep devoid of any trace of hand or foothold. That above was as formidable; a carved overhang moist with condensation pearling the near-mirror finish. Only the sides were left.

Dumarest moved to the right, stepped up to balance on the rail and, extending his arm, quested along the stone. He found nothing and moved to the other side, this time probing with his knife. The point found a crack, slipped into it, held for a moment then rasped free.

Back in the apartment he went into Angado's bedroom, found sheets, ripped them into strips to form a rope, lashed one end around his waist. On the balcony he tied the free end to the rail and, mounting it, tried again. This time the knife held and he swung from the rail on its support. His left hand found a hold and he heaved, boots scrabbling for purchase. A few inches and he rested before moving again. Farther out this time, a little higher, the knife coming free to find a new hold. Up and along again to halt as the rope tightened at his waist.

The moment of decision as wind tore at his hair and the roar of falling water echoed in his ears.

To free himself from the rope was to risk everything on his ability to climb to the upper edge of the chasm. avoid the men waiting there and make his escape in some way. To return to the apartment was to reenter the trap Avro had constructed; a sealed place from which there was only one exit and that guarded by watchful men.

Taken, he would be held, questioned, his mind probed to the last cell. He would be stripped of all knowledge then discarded as so much useless gargage. To attempt to climb was to risk falling to the rocks below. A quick death against one of long-drawn torment.

A choice made for him as rock crumbled beneath his boot and the knife slipped free to send him falling to halt with a jerk at the end of the rope. Thrusting the blade back into his boot he climbed hand over hand back to the balcony.

On the floor Avro stirred; a crippled spider tormented by savage dreams. From the room of bizarre decorations came the rolling echo of drums as Wynne Tewson pounded feebly at the door.

She was pale, lips almost bloodless, eyes marred by a yellowish tinge. The silver helmet of her hair was mussed and a bruise showed livid on her left cheek. She fought against Dumarest's arms as he dragged her into the bathroom, stripping her before holding her beneath the stinging shower. As she dried herself, shivering from the icy spray, he searched her clothing, pocketing the keys he found.

"You bastard!" Dressed, she glared at him. "You smart, know-it-all bastard!"

"Shut your mouth."

"Lying to me. Kissing me—then shoving me into that gas. And then what? Woke Angado, I suppose and used him to help you. Now you want me to do the same. Well, you can go to hell!"

"You'll go first." He grabbed her arm and dragged her into the main salon. "Over the edge and down to the rocks." He pointed at the open door of the balcony. "You want that?"

"You wouldn't—"

"What have I to lose?" He was curt in his interruption. "Men are waiting on the surface to take me. If they do it's my life. You tried to trap me—why the hell should I consider you? Make your choice. You help or you go over." He pulled her toward the opening. To where the roar of falling water filled the air. "What's it to be?"

A choice that was no choice at all. She looked at the water, his eyes, the mouth that had grown cruel.

"I'll help, but what can I do? This place is like a prison."

With men waiting outside on guard. By why did they wait? How long had they been ordered to stand by before taking action? Who would give the order for them to move in?

Avro stirred again and Dumarest guessed the answer. One verified as he stripped off the scarlet robe to reveal the mechanism clipped inside. A small transmitter which, when activated, would bring the others crashing in. The gas had worked too quickly for the cyber to have used it—a failure that gave Dumarest a chance.

"It won't work." Wynne stared as Dumarest donned the scarlet robe. "You'll never pass for a cyber."

"Maybe not."

"What happened to him?" She glanced at Perotto lying in a pool of blood that had drained from his mouth. "Did you do that?"

"He killed Angado."

"So you killed him?"

She shivered as he nodded, knowing he would kill her with the same lack of compassion if she thwarted him. As he would kill anyone who presented a threat or who had done him injury. An attribute she had sensed when lying in his arms. Even when sharing a mutual passion and, remembering it, she felt a sudden desire.

"Earl! Earl, you can trust me!"

Dumarest ignored her, cutting free the rope still hanging from the balcony, dipping a portion of it into the carmine pool beside Perotto's head, winding it around his skull to form a blood-stained bandage which covered most of his face. With talc from the bathroom he whitened his features and stooped for the robe to sweep the floor.

Scarlet identified a cyber, one hurt, his face almost invisible beneath the bandage and the drawn cowl.

"Earl?"

He said, "The way out is by the elevator or the stairs. The stairs will be guarded so we'll use the elevator. I'll lean on you and you'll explain to anyone who asks that I was hurt by the man I came for. He's still downstairs gased and helpless."

She was bitter at his rejection. "Then what? We take wings and fly?"

"One thing at a time. First we get out. Unless we do that the rest doesn't matter."

"Not to you," she agreed. "But I'd just as soon stay here."

"As a corpse?" Dumarest stepped close to her, the knife glimmering in his hand. Steel as hard as the determination stamped on his face. "I'm fighting for my life, girl. Remember that. Cross me and you'll be dead. The same if you betray me. The same if you don't cooperate. Now let's get going."

The elevator sighed down and to a halt at Wynne's signal. It held a man who went down beneath the smashing impact of Dumarest's knife, the pommel a hammer throwing the man into unconsciousness. Blood would have betrayed the deception; the missing man could prove an asset. Dumarest dragged him from the elevator before locking the woman to him with his left arm, his right hand with the knife slipping close to prick her flesh through the clothing.

"He was sent to stand guard over Dumarest," he said. "If anyone should ask that's what you tell them. Volunteer the information if they are suspicious but don't go into too much detail."

"Dumarest?"

"Just do as I say." She winced as the point dug deeper. "Up now."

The door slid shut and the elevator moved upward. As it came to a halt Dumarest sagged even more, throwing his weight against the woman, twisting to hide the blade he held against her.

"Master!" The acolyte was concerned, stepping forward as he saw the figure in the scarlet robe. "Master, are you hurt?"

"A head injury." Wynne answered the question. "Please step to one side."

Tupou obeyed, checking the empty elevator, stepping toward it.

"The man is guarding Dumarest." Wynne spoke quickly, conscious of the knife at her side. "Inform your master that he is ready to be taken."

His master? Ishaq had his own aides but Tupou was assigned to Avro. A thing the cyber would have known if not the woman, but why hadn't he ordered her to summon aid if he was hurt? Expecially when his acolyte was so close.

Dumarest whispered, "Tell him to report to the other cyber." He had seen the glow of the scarlet robe. "You will attend me until Dumarest is taken. Hurry!"

A matter of efficiency which the acolyte could appreciate. Avro was in no immediate danger but the quarry must be taken at all costs. And, if there was doubt, Ishaq could settle it.

He came forward, impatient at the delay, the need to accede to Avro's decision. The operation had been badly conducted; too much time had passed since Dumarest had entered the trap. He should now be safely contained. As it was he had managed to hurt Avro and done who knew what else?

"Wait." He called after the pair now moving toward the woman's raft. "Cyber Avro. A moment."

One in which the masquerade would be exposed and what would happen to her for having aided the deception? Wynne felt the sudden rising of panic.

"No!" She twisted away with desperate strength, breaking Dumarest's hold tearing herself from the blade at her side.

"He isn't Avro! He's the man you want! Dumarest! He's Dumarest!"

The betrayal he had feared. Now only speed could save him. Dumarest straightened, running toward the raft, his hand diving into a pocket and finding the keys he'd taken from Wynne's clothing.

A precaution justified as she called, "He can't get away. It's locked. I've—" Her tone changed as she discovered the theft. "Get to the other raft. Chase him. Move, damn you! Move!"

Orders followed as Ishaq gestured obedience. Dumarest reached Wynne's vehicle as the cyber and his men climbed into their own, the woman with them, eager to demonstrate her loyalty.

It lifted as Dumarest fumbled with the keys, finding the right one almost too late, jerking the raft up from beneath the shadow of the other. A beam struck the rear edge and metal flowed from the point of impact. More as the laser quested for the generator to wreck it and bring down the raft. Shots which ended as Dumarest sent it darting forward to hover over the waterfall, hanging poised as the other vehicle came up behind him, men leaning over the rail ready to jump when given the chance.

As it drew close Dumarest hit the controls.

Fire streamed from the rear of his raft; the roaring torch of the auxiliary burners Wynne had demonstrated during the night. Livid flames bathed the other raft with their fury. Searing those it contained like ants in a blowtorch. Sending them to fall into the chasm of the waterfall as Dumarest rose toward the sky, to freedom, to the man who could tell him how to find Earth.

Presenting JOHN NORMAN in DAW editions . . .